THE CONTRACTOR AND THE ENGINEER

a graphic novel

by

anil cs rao

AUTHOR BIO

Anil CS Rao was born in Hyderabad in 1964.at Neelofar Hospital. In 1969, his family moved to The States for the sake of his parent's career as medical doctors. He worked in civil service in The States as an electrical engineer until early retirement in 2003.

He holds an MFA in Creative Writing (English) from National University based in San Diego, California, and a bachelor's in engineering from Pratt Institute in Brooklyn New York.

From 2003 onwards - he shifted his focus from the engineering line to writing fiction, poetry, and graphic novels. Three of his initial forays were placed in the Top 17 comics by FHM (India) Magazine. He is currently collaborating with Hollywood actress/celebrity Ms. Kathy Garver (www.kathygarver.com) on a series of books released in English and Telugu languages.

You can read more about Anil CS Rao on his website: https://anilcsrao.com.

WASHINGTON SQUARE PARK, LOWER MANHATTAN - JULY 17, 1991 - ANAND AND PRINNY MEET UP AFTER WORK ...
SOFTENS YOUR HANDS WHILE YOU WASH THE DISHES - I BET IT DOES !
... FEEL LIKE RUFFLING PRINNY'S FEATHERS
PRINNY ...
REMEMBER THAT EX BF WHO PUNCHED YOU? THEN FLED THROUGH THE FIRE ESCAPE THROUGH MY OPEN WINDOW?
IS HE STILL IN PRISON FOR ASSAULT WITH AN INTENT TO MURDER?
WTF !

GOD ! WILL YOU LOOK AT THE PRICE - I COULD HAVE DONE THIS WITH A PAINT BALL GUN !
ANAND - I KNOW YOU'RE QUITE A PHILISTINE - BUT DO TRY AND SAY NICE THINGS ABOUT MY ROOMMATES ART !
HEIDI ! WE WERE ADMIRING YOUR WORKS ! THIS IS MY FRIEND ANAND -WE LIVED NEXT DOOR IN THAT COOP ON THOMPSON
MADAM HEIDI: I BOW TO YOU AND THE ARTISTIC GENIOUS OF PRINNY'S CURATION OF YOUR MASTERPIECES !

YOUR WORKS - HAVE MOVED ME PROFOUNDLY HEIDI JI !
MORE PROBABLY THAT WINE MULTIPLYING THE EFFECT OF HIS PILLS!
ANAND HAS OFFERED TO HELP YOU CLOSE UP THE SHOW TODAY - I HAVE TO GET BACK TO MY PLACE TO DO THE SAME ...
HEIDI : I'M SORRY - MAYBE IT WAS THE WINE - BUT I COULDN'T GET THE JIST OF THE WORKS PRESENTED ...
LOL !

ANAND : ARE YOU GAY? CAN'T YOU RECOGNIZE WHEN AN AMERICAN WOMAN IS TRYING TO FLIRT WITH YOU? THE STRANGE THING IS I AM GAY - AND MARRIED TO PRINNY - BUT AM SOMEHOW DRAWN TO YOU ...
PRINNY INFORMED ME THAT YOU MAY BE WILLING TO HELP US HAVE A CHILD ...
A HALF TELUGU BRAHMIN'S AND HALF GERMAN CATHOLIC ... HITLER WOULD BE PROUD ! BUT IF HE FOUND OUT WHY ... THAT KID WOULD BE SENT TO ONE OF HIS GAS CHAMBERS!

YOU KNOW PRINNY AND I WILL DO EVERYTHING WE CAN TO BRING UP THE CHILD WITH A PROGRESSIVE, OPEN MIND
I HAVE TO LEAVE FOR INDIA IN TWO DAYS FOR SOME FAMILY RELATED BUSINESS - I WILL LET YOU KNOW UPON MY RETURN IN 3 WEEKS
PRINNY AND I WILL HAVE ALL THE LEGAL WORK DONE PRIOR TO YOUR RETURN - AND ANAND - I WOULD PREFER THIS TO BE A "NATURAL" INSEMINATION - NOT AN IUI AS IS THE CASE WHEN THE DONOR IS ANONYMOUS
DEVUDU: HOW DO I GET MYSELF INTO THINGS LIKE THIS?

NAMASKARAM ANAND GARU: WE FINALLY MEET AFTER ALL THESE MONTHS OF EMAILS AND POSTCARDS!
IT'S HARD BEING SINGLE IN AMERICA - IN THAT IN ADDITION TO DOING MY JOB - I HAVE TO TAKE CARE OF LAUNDRY AND COOKING MY OWN MEALS !
SO HOW WOULD YOU IMGINE I WOULD LIKE TO COOK YOUR MEALS EVERYDAY !
AND HOW BIG IS THAT "TUBE STEAK" BETWEEN YOUR LEGS ?

LISTEN - YOU'RE ONLY HERE IN INDIA 3 WEEKS - AND I WISH YOU TO UNDERSTAND ME HENCEFORTH FROM THIS FIRST DAY ...
SO NOW THAT WE HAVE MET - I NEED YOU TO KNOW A LITTLE BIT ABOUT ME PRIOR TO A FORMAL ENGAGEMENT
WITH MY UNCLE'S BLESSINGS - I'LL TAKE YOU ON A "FIRST DATE" TOMORROW MORNING ...

I THINK I RECOGNIZE THE ARTIST - MF HUSSAIN?
THEY ARE FAKES - I HAD THEM MADE FROM PHOTOS ...
NEVER BELIEVE ANYTHING - UNTIL YOU'RE ABSOLUTELY SURE IT'S REAL - MY LATE DAD'S LAST WORDS TO ME

ROOPA TAKES ANAND ON THEIR FIRST DATE ...
APOLOGY FOR THE MEANS OF CONVEYANCE ...
THIS 2 WHEELER IS ACTUALLY SHARED BY MY MY UNCLE AND I ....
I MEAN SERIOUSLY - NOW THAT I FINISHED COLLEGE IN BOMBAY AND KNOW ABSOLUTELY NOONE HERE IN VIZAG - WHERE AM I REALLY TO GO ? I DON'T GET AROUND MUCH ANYWAY AS YOU CAN GUESS ...MY UNCLE NEEDING ASSISTANCE MOST OF HIS WAKING TIME ...

REACHING THEIR DESTINATION OUTSIDE THE CITY ...
JUST 30 MINUTES AWAY FROM THE COASTAL ANDHRA HINTERLAND ...I WAS A GEOGRAPHY STUDENT AT BOMBAY UNIVERSITY - UNFORTUNATELY MY MARKS WERE NOT HIGH ENOUGH TO GET INTO A REPUTABLE MA - HENCE I HAD NO OPTION BUT TO COME LIVE WITH MY UNCLE HERE IN MY NATIVE VIZAG AFTER MY FOLKS BOTH PASSED AWAY ONE YEAR BACK ...
THE POPULATION IS MUCH LESS DENSE ... HENCE THE POLLUTION AND HYGIENE - AND YES, MOST IMPORTANTLY - THE COST OF LIVING IS SOMEWHAT OF AN IMPROVMENT OVER BOMBAY WHERE I GREW UP WITH MY FOLKS IN MATUNGA

MY LATE DAD OULD BRING US HERE WHEN WE ERE SMALL FOR ICS ...THAT NASTY UNGER BROTHER ROTHER OF MINE WAS ACTUALLY NICE TO ME THOSE DAYS!
I REALLY DIDN'T REALLY SHED TOO ANY TEARS WHEN MY ROTHER PASSED AWAY FEW YEARS BEFORE I FINISHED COLLEGE IN BOMBAY ...
HE FELL IN WITH THE WRONG PEOPLE - DRANK HIMSELF TO DEATH ... KIND OF SAD IN A WAY ... I MEAN THINGS COULD HAVE CHANGED DRAMATICALLY AND WE COULD BE ACTUALLY BE GETTING ALONG IF HE WAS ALIVE NOW ...

ALL THIS ANCIENT HISTORY MAY BE INTERESTING - BUT THAT IS NOT WHY I BROUGHT YOU TO THIS SECLUDED SPOT "FAR FROM THE MADDENING CROWD" -
AND I CAN ASSURE YOU - I HAVE NO INTENTIONS OF INTIMACY - ONLY AN ENVIRONMENT IN WHICH I CAN LET MY GUARD DOWN AND BE CANDID ...
ANAND - I HAVE TO DISCUSS A REQUIREMENT I HAVE BEFORE WE CAN PROCEED ANY FURTHER - AND I AM SORRY - IF YOU CAN NOT AGREE I AM AFRAID WE CAN GO NO FURTHER AND MUST PART AS FRIENDS ...
OKAY - SPEAK - I AM LISTENING ...

I'VE SEEN SO MANY MARRIAGES - WITHIN MY FAMILY RELATIONS AND MY FRIENDS IN COLLEGE -
MORPH INTO SOMETHING - WELL - AWFUL ...
I MEAN GROWN UP ADULTS - GOING AT EACH OTHER LIKE LITERAL ANIMALS IN A CAGE ...
SO ANAND ...
PLEASE UNDERSTAND WHERE I AM COMING FROM ...

I HAVE - THEREFORE - A REQUIREMENT BEFORE WE CAN FINALIZE OUR MARRIAGE
I NEED YOU TO SIGN AN AGREEMENT ...
BASICALLY STATING THAT AT ANY POINT - EITHER OF US FEELS COMPELLED TO TERMINATE OUR MARRIAGE ... EVEN IF THE OTHER PARTY FEELS THAT THE DIFFERENCES MAY BE RECONCILABLE -
... UNLESS THIS AGREEMENT IS SIGNED BY BOTH OF US - AND IS ATTESTED BY LEGAL AUTHORITY BINDING IN BOTH INDIA AND THE STATES ... WE SHOULD PART AS FRIENDS NOW ... A "TALL ORDER" AS YOU AMERICANS MAY PUT IT?

AND ANAND - WITHIN A FEW MINUTES OF CONSIDERATION - DESPITE ROOPA'S PLEA TO THINK OVERNIGHT - ACCEPTED THE BASIC CONDITION OF ROOPA'S PROPOSED PRENUPTIAL CONTRACT : THE COUPLE WOULD GO THEIR SEPARATE WAYS INDEPENDENT OF THE LEGAL SYSTEM IN EITHER INDIA OR THE STATES - IF EITHER ROOPA OR ANAND FIND THEMSELVES IN A POSITION WHERE THEY FEEL BETTER OFF SEPARATED FROM THE OTHER ... AND THAT COULD BE A SUBJECTIVE OPINION NOT BASED ON IRRECONCILABLE DIFFERENCES ...
WELL - IN ANY CASE - I WILL WAIT UNTIL TOMORROW MORNING TO INFORM MY UNCLE AND FAMILY - AND IT OFFICIAL ...
I THINK I MAY MAY HAVE MENTIONED IT TO YOU - BEING A FELLOW BRAHMIN - I THOUGHT WE WOULD HAVE A TRADITIONAL TEMPLE WEDDING ....
THE YOU CAN OFFICIALLY DEFLOWER ME THE NIGHT FOLLOWING ! ACTUALLY LOOKING FORWARD TO THAT!
(WOW!)

AT A LOCATION SOUTH OF VIZAG METRO:
THIS IS WHERE WE WILL HAVE OUR WEDDING TOMORROW - IT WAS A PROJECT FOR MY LATE DAD - A CIVIL ENGINEER - TO BUILD A TEMPLE FOR THE GENERAL PUBLIC
UNFORTUNATELY - HE PASSED AWAY BEFORE IT WAS COMPLETED - MY UNCLE RENTS IT OUT FOR MARRIAGE FUNCTIONS - "KALYANAMANTAPAM" - WHERE THE BRIDE & GROOM MAKE THE FIRST 7 STEPS INTO A HINDU MARRIAGE
I WARNED YOU ABOUT GIRLS WHO REQUEST TRADITIONAL HINDU MARRAIGES - AND YOU SAID: "I'LL TAKE MY CHANCES" !

SO BY TOMORROW AFTERNOON THE JARI'S WILL BE HERE AND WE WILL TAKE OUR VOWS AROUND THE HOLY FIRE ...
I DON'T KNOW ABOUT YOU - BUT I AM AS FRIGHTENED AS I AM EXCITED ... YOU KNOW: IT'S BEEN A DREAM SINCE CHILDHOOD TO GO TO THE TOP OF THE EMPIRE STATE BUILDING AND DO MY BEST FAY WRAY - WITH YOU PLAYING THE PART OF KING KONG !
SO - YOU SHAMELESS GORILLA: HOW ARE YOU PLANNING ON "TAKING " ME ON OUR FIRST NIGHT?
NO WORRIES ANAND : THE QUESTION CAN BE CONSIDERED A RHETORICAL ONE !
IT'S GETTING LATE: WHY NOT WE END THIS PRENUPTIAL MEETING - THE DOCUMENT OF THE OF THE SAME SIGNED AND SEALED - TO GO FOR A SILENT WALKING MEDITATION ... JUST THE SOUNDS OF THE OCEAN ...

ROOPA AND ANAND - ENGAGED FOR 1 WEEK - NOW TAKE THEIR LAST WALK PRIOR TO THE FOLLOWING DAY'S WEDDING ...
TOMORROW WE'LL SEND THE CAR TO YOUR HOTEL EARLY MORNING - AT AROUND 5 AM
ONLY MY UNCLE AND THE PUJARI WILL BE PRESENT - I DON'T HAVE MANY FRIENDS HERE IN VIZAG - AND I DIDN'T HAVE TIME TO INVITE MY FRIENDS AND CLASSMATES IN BOMBAY ...

MY BELOVED, OUR LOVE BECAME FIRM BY WALKING ONE STEP WITH ME. YOU WILL OFFER ME THE FOOD AND BE HELPFUL IN EVERY WAY. I WILL CHERISH YOU AND PROVIDE FOR THE WELFARE AND HAPPINESS OF YOU AND OUR CHILDREN.
THIS IS MY HUMBLE SUBMISSION TO YOU, MY LORD. YOU KINDLY GAVE ME RESPONSIBILITY OF THE HOME, FOOD AND TAKING CHARGE OF THE FINANCE. I PROMISE YOU THAT I SHALL DISCHARGE ALL RESPONSIBILITIES FOR THE WELFARE OF THE FAMILY AND CHILDREN.
SAPTAPADI
LITERALLY TRANSLATING TO SEVENSTEPS IN SANSKRIT) ...
REFERS TO THE SEVEN PROMISES OF MARRIAGE THAT A BRIDE AND GROOM TAKE WITH EACH STEP JUST LIKE THE VOWS THAT ARE SAID IN A CHRISTIAN CEREMONY. THIS IS ONE OF THE MOST IMPORTANT RITUALS IN A HINDU WEDDING.
THE SECOND STEP...
MY BELOVED, YOU HAVE NOW WALKED THE SECOND STEP WITH ME. FILL MY HEART WITH STRENGTH AND COURAGE AND TOGETHER WE SHALLPROTECT THE HOUSEHOLD AND CHILDREN.
MY LORD, IN YOUR GRIEF I SHALL FILL YOUR HEART WITH STRENGTH. IN YOUR HAPPINESS, I SHALL REJOICE. I PROMISE YOU THAT I WILL PLEASE YOU ALWAYS WITH SWEET WORDS AND TAKE CARE OF THE FAMILY AND CHILDREN AND YOU SHALL LOVE ME ALONE AS YOUR WIFE.

THIRD STEP ....
MY BELOVED NOW YOU HAVE WALKED THREE STEPS WITH ME. BY VIRTUE OF THIS, OUR WEALTH AND PROSPERITY ARE BOUND TO GROW. I SHALL LOOK UPON ALL OTHER WOMEN AS MY SISTERS. TOGETHER, WE WILL EDUCATE OUR CHILDREN AND MAY THEY LIVE LONG.
MY LORD I WILL LOVE YOU WITH SINGLE MINDED DEVOTION AS MY HUSBAND I WILL TREAT ALL OTHER MEN AS MY BROTHERS. MY DEVOTION TO YOU IS OF A CHASTE WIFE AND YOU ARE MY JOY. THIS IS MY COMMITMENT AND PLEDGE TO YOU.
4RTH STEP ...
MY BELOVED IT IS A GREAT BLESSING THAT YOU HAVE WALKED FOUR STEPS WITH ME. YOU HAVE BROUGHT AUSPICIOUSNESS AND SACREDNESS INTO MY LIFE. MAY WE BE BLESSED WITH OBEDIENT AND NOBLE CHILDREN. MAY THEY BE BLESSED WITH LONG LIFE.
MY LORD I WILL DECORATE YOU FROM YOUR FEET UP WITH FLOWERS, GARLANDS AND ANOINT YOU WITH SANDAL WOOD PASTE AND FRAGRANCE. I WILL SERVE YOU AND PLEASE YOU IN EVERY WAY.

5TH STEP ...
MY LORD I SHARE BOTH IN YOUR JOYS AND SORROWS. YOUR LOVE WILL MAKE ME TRUST AND HONOR YOU. I WILL CARRY OUT YOUR WISHES.
MY BELOVED NOW THAT YOU HAVE WALKED THE FIVE STEPS WITH ME, YOU HAVE ENRICHED MY LIFE. MAY GOD BLESS YOU. MAY OUR LOVED ONES LIVE LONG AND SHARE IN OUR PROSPERITY.
THE 6TH STEP ...
MY LORD IN ALL ACTS OFRIGHTEOUSNESS, IN MATERIAL PROSPERITY AND IN EVERY FORM OF ENJOYMENT AND DIVINE ACTS, I PROMISE YOU THAT I SHALL PARTICIPATE AND SHALL ALWAYS BE WITH YOU.
MY BELOVED YOU HAVE FILLED MY HEART WITH HAPPINESS BY WALKING SIX STEPS WITH ME. MAY YOU FILL MY HEART WITH GREAT JOY AND PEACE FROM TIME TO TIME.

AT THE CONCLUSION OF THE THE 7TH FINAL STEP ...
MY BELOVED AS YOU WALKED THE SEVEN STEPS WITH ME, OUR LOVE AND FRIENDSHIP BECAME ETERNAL. WE EXPERIENCED SPIRITUAL UNION IN GOD NOW YOU HAVE BECOME COMPLETELY MINE AND I OFFER MY LIFE TO YOU. OUR MARRIAGE WILL BE FOREVER.
MY LORD AS PER THE LAW OF GOD AND THE HOLY SCRIPTURES [VEDAS] I HAVE BECOME YOUR SPOUSE. WHATEVER PROMISES WE GAVE, WE HAVE SPOKEN WITH PURE MIND WE WILL BE TRUTHFUL TO EACH OTHER IN ALL THINGS. WE WILL LOVE EACH OTHER FOR EVER.
ANAND - I STILL NEED TO GIVE YOU SOMETHING VERY IMPORTANT BEFORE YOU LEAVE TONIGHT .. LETS MEET I N AN HOUR

THE DAY AFTER THE WEDDING - AND THEIR "FIRST NIGHT" ...
SO ANAND ...
HOW DOES IT FEEL? A NEWLY MARRIED MAN?
ANAND - LET'S SIT DOWN - I NEED TO GIVE YOU SOMETHING RATHER SPECIAL ...
OVER THERE - THERE SEEMS TO BE SOME SORT OF SHRINE ...

THIS MANGALASUTRA - I HAD IT MADE FROM THE GOLD FROM YOUR MOTHERS - AN UPDATED VERSION ...
I COMBINED THE REMAINING GOLD WITH A DIAMOND OWNED BY MY LATE FATHER ...
WHAT INGENUITY!
I DIDN'T HAVE MUCH TIME GIVEN YOU'RE LEAVING BACK TO NEW YORK TOMORROW ...
AND THOUGH MY DESIGN SENSE IS OKAY - I HAD TO TAKE THE JEWELER'S SUGGESTION - AND WELL - I HOPE YOU'LL WEAR IT 24/7 - AND ALWAYS KEEP ME IN YOUR HEART OF HEARTS WHILE I WAIT HERE TO BE CALLED TO JOIN YOU ...

OKAY ANAND ...
HERE IT IS ...
ROOPA - THANK YOU, THANK YOU FROM THE DEPTHS OF MY HEART ...

JUST AFTER THE WEDDING AT THE TEMPLE - ROOPA MEETS ANAND AT HIS HOTEL - NOW ANAND'S LEGAL WIFE
GOD! THAT WAS TORTURE -I REALLY SHOULD SEE DOCTOR BEFORE I JOIN HIM IN NEW YORK!
I HAVE TO REPORT AT THE AIRPORT FOR THE FLIGHT TO BOMBAY IN 2 HOURS
ANAND - I'M REALLY SORRY ABOUT THIS - AS I SAID - IT WOULD GET KIND OF MESSY AS I'M IN THE MIDDLE OF A PERIOD CYCLE ,,,
BUT HEY - I CAN STILL MASSAGE YOUR PRIVATE PART AND YOU CAN RELEASE ...
I DID IT ONCE FOR THAT BUTT HOLE I WAS DATING WHEN I WAS A STUDENT AT ELPHINSTONE
ROOPA...PLEASE ...I HAVE TO START PACKING FOR THE FLIGHT ...

JULY 30TH, 1991 - ON THE LAST LEG OF THE JOURNEY BETWEEN INDIA AND JFK ON AN AIR INDIA FLIGHT ...
VEG OR NON-VEG?
WHATEVER - NO PREFERENECE
THE FLIGHT'S ALMOST EMPTY - SO YOU CAN HAVE ANYTHING YOU WISH - BUT I SUGGEST THE VEG - LITTLE LESS SPICY AND YOUR KARMA WON'T BE HARMED ...
ARE YOU FLYING FOR BUSINESS PURPOSES?
NO - SOME PERSONAL BUSINESS ...
I WAS ABOUT TO SAY - YOUR EMPLOYER MUST BE A CHEAPSKATE BOOKING YOU ON SEATS LIKE THIS - AGAIN - THE FLIGHT'S EMPTY - FEEL FREE TO USE THE ADJACENT SEATS TO SLEEP ...

LISTEN - MY NAME IS ZARINA - I REALLY DON'T HAVE A LOT OF TIME TO EXPLAIN - YOU SEEM LIKE A COOL GUY AND NOT BAD ON THE EYES - MY GIRLFRIENDS AND I ARE ALWAYS SHORT ON CASH FOR SHOPPING AT CONWAY'S WHEN WE'RE ON LAYOVERS IN NEW YORK ...
I THINK YOU GET THE JIST - BEING A NEW YORKER - IF YOU COULD MEET US THIS SUNDAY AND TAKE US TO CONWAY'S BEFORE OUR FLIGHT BACK TO MUMBAI THE NEXT MORNING ...,
OKAY - I'M GOING TO GIVE YOU MY CARD - AND PLEASE DON'T SHARE IT WITH ANYONE - IT COULD GET INTO ME BIG TROUBLE - EVEN FIRED ...
???
SHIT ! THE CABIN CREW SUPERVISOR IS ON THE PROWL! BETTER GET THOSE MEALS OUT !

:10 AM
:0
OMPSON
TREET, NY NY
012
5:15 AM BLEEKER STEET
West 4 Street-Washington
Square Station A C E B D F M
Elevator at
W3 St & 6 Av
:20 AM
A BENEFIT OF BEING A CITY EMPLOYEE WAS BEING EXEMPT FROM FARES ON PUBLIC TRANSPORT - PROVIDED THE EMPLOYEE DISPLAY HIS BADGE ...
PAY YOUR FARE !!!

5:45 AM
ANAND – NOW THAT YOU HAVE A WIFE COMING TO JOIN SOON – YOU REALLY HAVE TO SLOW DOWN AND CONSIDER YOUR PRIORITIES ... YOU MAY THINK "MEHMET IS A JUST A STREET VENDOR" – BUT I HAPPEN TO MANAGE SEVERAL PROPERTIES IN JACKSON HEIGHTS .. IN ADDITION TO MY HOUSE IN WHITESTONE ...
SO IF AT SOME POINT YOU WISH TO GET OUT OF THAT ROACH INFESTED STUDIO IN THAT IMMORAL SECTION OF MANHATTAN TO SOMEPLACE WHERE A RESPECTABLE FAMILY MAN WOULD LIVE ...
5:47 AM

5:48 AM
LISTEN - I PUT MY CALLING CARD IN THE BAG - TAKE MY SINCERE ADVICE AND DO FIND A BETTER PLACE FOR YOUR NEST - IN HINDI: GHARONDA
5:50 AM
MEHMET - I APPRECIATE IT ...
5:53 AM
6 AM : 16TH FLOOR 1350 6TH AVENUE
ANAND: IT'S FRIDAY - SINCE YOU'RE TAKING THE DAY OFF AFTER LUNCH TODAY - PLEASE SUBMIT YOUR TIME CARD TO ME ASAP

MR ANAND ... !
WHEN WILL YOU STOP HOGGING THAT WORKSTATION AND PRETENDING YOU'RE WORKING? AND YES: I HEARD THAT RUMOR OF YOUR WIFE'S CONNECTION WITH THE BIG GUY UPSTAIRS ! BEING A AVID UNION ADVOCATE - THAT DOES'NT SCARE ME ONE BIT !
DARIUS: TO PUT VERY SIMPLY : FUCK OFF AND FUCK YOU ... WHY DON'T YOU GO HOME TO IRAN AND KISS THE AYATOLLAH'S ASSHOLE?

IT'S JUST AFTER LUNCHTIME FRIDAY AUGUST 14, 1991 MEGHAN CHOY, HEAD OF HR FOR THE CITY'S PW ENGINGEERING DEPARTMENT , AND CLASSMATE OF ANAND'S - BOTH HAVE TAKEN HALF THE DAY OFF TO MAKE A TRIP TO JONES BEACH STATE PARK - A 2 HOUR TRIP FROM ANAND'S BLUE GREEN COOP BUILDING ON 180 THOMPSON ...
HEY - THANKS FOR AGREEING TO COME - I JUST HAD TO GET YOU OUT OF THE CITY FOR A WHILE ...
I MEAN ANAND - THAT RUFUS YOU CREATED IN THE CADD ROOM THE OTHER DAY FIGHTING WITH THAT DARIUS CREEP ...
I KNOW - THIS IS A CITY JOB - BUT THAT SORT OF THING WILL EVENTUALLY GET YOU FIRED ...

LEAVING MANHATTAN VIA CANAL STREET ...
AND THE MANHATTAN BRIDGE ...
AND ONTO THE BROOKLY QUEENS EXPRESSWAY ...
IT SHOULD START BULIDING UP ON THE B.Q.E. AROUND NOW - BUT YOU CAN NEVER BE SURE WITH ALL THIS CONSTRUCTION SCHEDULED DURING THE SUMMER MONTHS ...

ROUND 2:30 PM THEY
PPROACH THE
NTRANCE TO JONES
EACH PARK ...
I GUESS IT'S SAFE TO PARK LIKE THIS - WE WON'T BE GONE FOR MORE THAN A HALF HOUR ...
SO ANAND ...
NOT SURE YOU'RE AWARE - THERE'S A RUMOR IN THE OFFICE YOUR WIFE IS RELATED TO OUR CHEIF ... AND I THINK THE SOURCE IS AT THE TOP ...
JONES BEACH

WOW - NO - I HAD NO CLUE - NOR DID ROOPA OR ANY OF HER RELATIONS MENTION THE CONNECTION ... I DO KNOW ROOPA'S LATE FATHER WAS SOME SORT OF BIG ENGINEER FOR THE INDIA GOVERNMENT PRIOR TO HIS RETIREMENT ALMOST 12 YEARS AGO ...
WELL - AS IT TURNS OUT : HER DAD AND OUR CHIEF WERE CLASSMATES IN ENGINEERING SCHOOL IN INDIA - BEST FRIENDS IN FACT ...

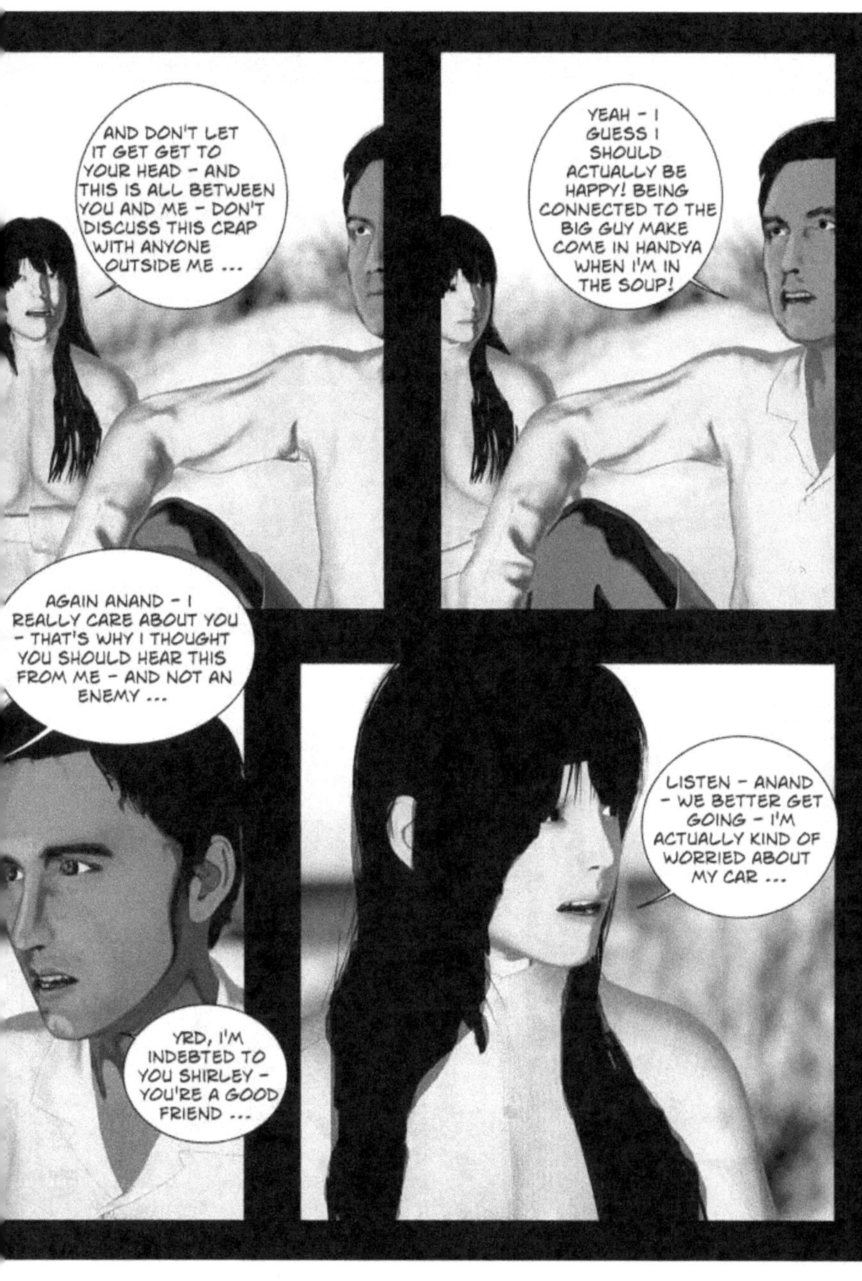
AND DON'T LET IT GET GET TO YOUR HEAD - AND THIS IS ALL BETWEEN YOU AND ME - DON'T DISCUSS THIS CRAP WITH ANYONE OUTSIDE ME ...
YEAH - I GUESS I SHOULD ACTUALLY BE HAPPY! BEING CONNECTED TO THE BIG GUY MAKE COME IN HANDYA WHEN I'M IN THE SOUP!
AGAIN ANAND - I REALLY CARE ABOUT YOU - THAT'S WHY I THOUGHT YOU SHOULD HEAR THIS FROM ME - AND NOT AN ENEMY ...
YRD, I'M INDEBTED TO YOU SHIRLEY - YOU'RE A GOOD FRIEND ...
LISTEN - ANAND - WE BETTER GET GOING - I'M ACTUALLY KIND OF WORRIED ABOUT MY CAR ...

SORRY - I THINK I LOST A SANDAL SOMEWHERE IN THAT DUNE ... MY FEET ARE BURNING !
SUCH A SWEET GUY - MY LOSS - THAT INDIAN BITCH'S GAIN ...
GOD! IF ONLY HAD I KNOWN ! I WOULD HAVE GRABBED MEGHAN CHOY SOME TIME AGO AND LED HER TO FOR A COURT MARRIAGE LONG TIME AGO ,,,
I MEAN : ANAND - WHAT'S THE MATTER WITH YOU?
ANAND - SINCE WHEN DID YOU BECOME SO STRAIGHT LACED LACED CONSERVATIVE?
ASK MY INDIAN ANCESTORS!

BACK AT 180 THOMPSON - SHIRELY FEELS SUDDENLY EMBOLDEN - "CARPE DIEM" AS PER SCHOOL DAYS AT GROTON ...
I WONDER WHAT HE PAYS FOR THIS DUMP ...
ANAND - DON'T MEAN TO SOUND CHEAP - BUT DON'T MEN GENERALLY ASK A WOMAN THEY LIKE UP TO THEIR PLACE AFTER A DATE? IF WE MAY CALL THIS THAT?
SALLY : BEING A MARRIED MAN - IT INDEED SOUNDS "CHEAP" ON YOUR PART - BUT I A SUCKER FOR CHEAP WOMEN IN GENERAL ...

ANAND - WHAT'S THE MATTER ? WHY DON'T YOU "TAKE" ME LIKE A REAL MAN WOULD? A REAL HOT BLOODED ASIAN ALBEIT ASIAN INDIAN MAN ...
MEGHAN
IF YOU DIDN'T ALREADY "GET IT" - I AM TAKEN - AND THE WIFE CAN ARRIVE ANYTIME .. WHENEVER HER VISA IS ISSUED ...
!!!

IT'S A BEAUTIFUL NIGHT ...
I DON'T GET IT ABOUT YOU INDIANS ...
I MEAN - YOU TAKE 3 WEEKS VACATION - FOR WHICH YOU SPENT 3 YEARS WORKING TO EARN ..
AND TO MY HUGE ISAPPOINTMENT - YOU RETURN A RRIED MAN ... IS ERE ANY HOPE FOR E LEFT ? A PART TIME LOVER PERHAPS?
LISTEN MEGHAN - THE FACT IS I AM NOW INDEED A MARRIED MAN - IT CAN'T GET ANY FURTHER THAN FOR US - AND LISTEN - TOMORROW IS A WORKING DAY AND YOU PROBABLY NEED TO GET HOME TO CHANGE FOR WORK EARLY MORNING ...

AT ANAND'S FORMER NEIGHBOR'S BAR ON THE CORNER OF HOUSTON AND SULLIVAN ..
ANAND ! YOU FU**ING SCUM BAG: YOU GO TO INDIA TELLING EVERYONE IT'S FOR SOME FAMILY BUSINESS -AND YOU RETURN A MARRIED MAN ! THAT'S SOME WEIRD KIND OF 'FAMILY BUSINESS' !
.. AND I DID GO TO A BARTENDING CLASS: YOU START SLURRING YOUR WORDS AFTER JUST ONE DRINK . I MEAN SHOULD YOU BE DRINKING WHILE ON THOSE PILLS THAT SHRINK WOMAN PRESCRIBED YOU?
FUNNY: THAT HEAD SHRINK : I SLEPT WITH HER THE OTHER DAY AFTER MY THERAPY SESSION -SHE THINKS I SHOULD BE HOSPITALIZED AND AM IN NO CONDITION FOR HAVING A WIFE DEPENDING ON ME .. THE WIFE ARRIVES IN A FEW WEEKS -AND THE ONLY FURNITURE I HAVE IS THAT FUTON I FOUND IN THE BASEMENT DUMP WHEN YOU LIVED NEXT DOOR TO ME AT THAT ROACH MOTEL I CALL MY APARTMENT .

YOU'RE NOT THE ONLY ONE WITH HOUSING PROBLEMS: I HAVE TO PUT UP WITH THAT POT DEALING ROOMATE -I MEAN -IF MY PLACE GETS RAIDED I'LL BE THROWN INTO JAIL AS HER ACCOMPLICE ! UNFORTUNATLE DEALING WEED IS HER ONLY SOURCE OF INCOME -AND I NEED NEXT MONTHS RENT TO PAY BILLS ..
!GOSH .. I DIDN'T KNOW ! ?
ANAND ..ANAND RAO LISTEN TO ME ..
YOU CAN CALL IT WHATEVER YOU WISH -: LOVE, LUST WHATEVER ...BUT DO KNOW WHETHER YOU'RE MARRIED OR JUST THE ADULTEREST BASTARD THAT YOU TRULY ARE -YOU CAN ALWAYS FIND ME WHEN YOU NEED ME -24/7 : PROMISE

WASHINGTON SQUARE PARK, NEW YORK CITY JUNE 1991 - SHORTLY AFTER ANAND'S RETURN FROM INDIA ...
WELL .. UNTIL YOUR MAIL ORDER INDIAN BRIDE ARRIVES - I PRETTY MUCH HAVE YOU TO MYSELF ...
BUT TIME IS LIMITED - I PRAY THAT THE US CONSULATE IN HYDERABAD DENY HER VISA BEING THAT SHE IS A GOLD DIGGER - AND JUST LOOKING FOR A GREEN CARD ...
IT'S LIKE: WHY BUY THE COW WHEN YOU GET THE MILK FOR FREE (ME!)

WELL- THIS IS ONE THING I DO MISS: MY BUILDING DOESN'T HAVE A LAUNDRY ROOM - WE HAVE TO GO TO ONE OF THOSE LAUNDROMATS OR USE THOSE CHINESE LAUNDRY PLACES: GETS EXPENSIVE
HEIDI WAS HEART BROKEN WHEN YOU RETURNED FROM INDIA - MARRIED AND UNABLE TO HELP HER HAVE A KID WITH ME
YOU SIMPLY WON'T UNDERSTAND THE ODD MORALITY OF INDIANS -I LEFT NEW YORK AS AMERICAN - AND RETURNED NOT ONLY "MARRIED" BUT A PERSON WITH THE MORALS ASSOCIATED WITH BEING INDIAN
ANAND - IS LIFE SOME SORT OF PETTY GAME IN WHICH OTHER HUMAN BEINGS ARE SIMPLY IGNORED FOR WHAT THEY ARE? HUMAN BEINGS WITH EMOTIONS AND A HEART? I MEAN ANAND !

ANAND: I PRESCRIBED YOU THAT PILL KLONOPIN TO RELIEVE SOME OF THE ANXIETY YOU WERE EXPERIENCING WHILE WAITING FOR YOUR SPOUSE IN INDIA TO JOIN YOU ...I EXPLICITLY WARNED YOU THAT THAT PILL IS AN ALCOHOL POTENTIATOR ...
WHY DON'T YOU ASK ME? I'LL GIVE IT TO YOU!
AND THAT'S NOT THE ONLY ISSUE : THESE DAYS I FIND MY SEXUAL URGE UNCONTROLABLE ... I ACTUALLY AM A PATRON OF A BROTHEL ON THE EAST SIDE OF MANHATTAN ..
THE REASON I AM NOT REMORSEFUL - I LEARNED THAT MY SPOUSE IS IN A RELATIONSHIP WITH ONE OF HER FELLOW STUDENTS AT THE PRATT INSTITUTE TO WHICH I AM PAYING FOR HER TO COMPLETE AN MFA
ANAND: I COME FROM A GERMAN CATHOLIC BACKGROUND WHEREIN ADULTERY IS A MORTAL SIN ..NONETHELESS I WOULD BE TAKING A CHANCE + POSSIBLY LOSE MY LICENSE TO PRACTICE.
I AM TAKING A RISK ASKING YOU .. BUT KEEP AN OPEN MIND ..

SO DOCTOR : YOU REALL THINK A GOOD FUCK WOULD BE MUCH MORE EFFECTIVE THAN ELECTRO CONVULSIVE THERAPY .
I LIVE IN THIS SAME BUILDING - WHY NOT WE HANG OUT THERE? LISTEN INSTEAD OF PAYING SOMEONE I CAN GIVE IT TO YOU FREE . AND YES I COULD INDEED LOSE MY LICENSE TO PRACTICE AS A DOCTOR
WELL: I NEVER HAD BEEN TURNED ON LIKE I HAVE WITH THIS ANAND DUDE 'WELL: I MAY LOSE MY LICENSE - BUT WHAT THE HELL DOES THE ALMIGHTY WISH ME TO DO?
WELL: AS SOON AS YOU WALK OUT OF THIS OFFICE -WE ARE NO LONGER IN A DOCTOR PATIENT RELATIONSHIP
SURE: UNDERSTOOD
OKAY ANAND - WHAT WE JUST DID IS AGAINST THE NORM FOR THE RELATIONSHIP OF A 'SHRINK' AND HIS OR HER RELATIONSHIP WITH THE PATIENT
BUT UNDERSTAND - THE OTHER SIDE HAS NEEDS TO - AND I MYSELF HAVE SURVIVED EPISODES OF DEPRESSION

GABE !
I AM AWARE YOU'RE LEAVING US SOON ..BUT YOU GET 'BIG BUCKS' TO WORK - NOT SOCIALIZE!
OF COURSE JOEL WHAT WOULD LIFE BE WITHOUT "BIG BUCKS TO GET MY EYEGLASSES REPAIRED?
WHY YOU SON OF A...
BOY! GABE AND JOEL ARE AT EACH OTHER'S THROATS!

YEAH KWAME -EVER SINCE HIS TRANSFER TO YOUR DEPT. BECAME OFFICIAL HE'S BEEN REALLY GIVING JOEL THE BUSINESS!
YES ANAND : I KNOW HOW MUCH YOU WANTED THAT POSITION -BUT I MAY BE THE BIG MAN DOWNSTAIRS - BUT YOUR BOSS - BUT MCABE IS 3 LEVELS ABOVE ME
ACTUALLY: I LIKED THE OTHER ONE BETTER ...
YEAH SHE'S THE ONLY REASON I WANTED THAT TRANSFER -SO I COULD KEEP AN EYE ON HER NOW AND THEN ...RATHER THAN BE CHAINED HERE IN MIDTOWN ..

WELL GABE: WELCOME TO THE WORLD OF FIELD ENGINEERING ... YOU'VE GOTTA BE ON TOP OF ANYTHING AND EVERYTHING HERE IN CONSTRUCTION PHASE - IRA THE CONTRACTOR WAS HOSPITALIZED LAST WEEK: BLACK LUNGS FROM THE TRACK DUST ... ARE YOU SURE YOU WANNA TRADE THAT NICE OFFICE FOR THIS?
LISTEN KWAME - EVERY MORNING I HAVE TO DEAL WITH ASSHOLE JOEL GETTING ON MY CASE - FOR THIS MEASLY SALARY HE'S EXPECTING THE MOON
ANAND: HEY SORRY YOU DIDN'T GET THIS POSITION: HAD YOU BEEN LIKE ME - A LOAFER IN LOAFER'S PARADISE - MAYBE THEY WOULD HAVE LET YOU GO HERE ...

YOU KNOW: IT'S LIKE THAT DIRE STRAITS TUNE: "MONEY FOR NOTHING AND THE CHICKS FOR FREE" !
OKAY - THIS IS THE POINT WE NEED YOUR DESIGN: A FEED FOR THE SIGNAL ENCOSURE AHEAD - IT'S BEEN MALFUNCTIONING AS OF LATE
AFTER YOU TAKE YOUR NOTES - BOTH YOU AND I GET TO GO HOME - IT'S ONLY 1 PM AFTER THE TIME WE TAKE LUNCH IN THE OFFICE .. NICE HUH?

ANAND: I AM KIND OF CURIOUS ...
I SEE ALL THESE WOMEN FALLING OVER BACKWARDS HERE IN NEW YORK ...
AND YOU TRAVERSE HALFWAY AROUND THE WORLD AND RETURN MARRIED TO A GIRL YOU'VE ONLY HAVE KNOWN IN PERSON FOR 3 WEEKS ..
I MEAN: YOU'VE BEEN IN AMERICA SINCE GRA SCHOOL AT NEW YORK POLY ...

I DON'T KNOW: THIS IS MY FAVORITE MANTRA: IN TELUGU : NAA KARMA KALAPOYINTHI
WE HAVE A COMMON THEME WITH RESPECT TO RELIGION: GOD SEES ALL - EVERY INFLECTION OF OUR THOUGHTS AND ACTIONS - AND REWARDS OR PUNISHES US BASED ON THESE ...
ANAND - I HAD A YARMULKE ON MY HEAD ON THE LAST DAY ON THE JOB - I REALLY AM NOT THAT RELIGIOUS - BUT I WISHED TO EXHIBIT MY RELIGION IN THE CONTEXT OF MY ANTI SEMITIC SUPERVISORS - THAT ARAB STARKEST AND THAT IRISH DRUNK MC CABE

ANY WAY - I THINK I HAVE ENOUGH FIELD NOTES AT THIS POINT TO DO THE DESIGN ...
AND YES GABE: YOU CAN GO HOME - BUT I'M RETURNING TO THE OFFICE TO START ,Y PRELIMINARY DESIGN - AND NO WORRIES - I WON'T MENTION ANYTHING ABOUT YOU SPLITTING NOW
ANAND: YOU CAN SAY AS YOU WISH TO THOSE SHITHEADS IN THE OFFICE - I AM CITING OUR UNION RULES ... GO HOME AFTER FIELD WORK IS OVER ..

GOOD MORNING ANAND ! ANOTHER DAY IN PARADISE FOR ENGINEERS ! I'M BEING SARCASTIC!
I LIKE THS ONE ESPECIALLY THE TRADITIONAL OUTFITS !
YOU WANNA RENDEZ-VOUS WITH MEGHAN AND I OUTSIDE FOR A FEW PUFFS?
YEAH - WHY NOT? - THE BREAKS ARE AS PER UNION RULES

WILL YOU LOOK AT THAT!
WHEN IS ANAND GOING TO LEARN? WHERE THERE'S SMOKE ... MOST LIKELY THERE'S FIRE !
MORNING IN MANHATTAN - SMELL THOSE FRESH BAGELS !
WELL - TODAY AT NOON I HAVE A 'HOT DATE' WITH ANAND - I HOPE I CAN TELL HIM SOME NEWS THAT CAN EITHER BE GOOD OR BAD ...

WAKE UP HOMEGIRLS - LISTEN TO WHAT BROTHER GARY IS SAYING : BLACK FOLK NEED JUSTICE !
WLIB : THIS IS IMHOTEP GARY BYRD
HUEY: I LOVE YOU !
!!!
???
ENTERTAINMENT !
FLAKY NI**ER: HE'S BEEN SITTING ON THE WORK I GAVE HIM FOR OVER A WEEK NOW !

ATTENTION BROTHERS AND SISTERS -THIS YOUR COMRADE LARRY BYRD OF WLIB: I SMELL A SKUNK IN THE NEW YORK JUDICAL SYSTEM: THE WAR HAS JUST STARTED BETWEEN THE BLACK MAN AND THE LOCAL CRACKER NYPD AT HOWARD BEACH ..
WELL HOME GIRLS: IN PREPARTION FOR THIS COMING WAR I'M AXKING YOU TO CLEAN YOUSELVES UP. STOP EATING THAT PORK "AND" STOP WORSHIPPING THAT BEARDED CRACKER WHO DESCENDED FROM THE SKY!
BE THANKFUL TO THE UNION YOU HAVE A JOB!
AND LIKE DOCTOR BEN STATES CLEARLY: WE WON'T FEEL JUSTICE HAS BEEN DONE TO THE BLACK MAN UNTIL WE EACH GET THAT PROMISED 40 ACRES & A MULE!
AND HOMEGIRLS: WE WANT IT NOW! HOW LONG DO OUR PEOPLE HAVE TO SUFFER UNDER A REGIME HEADED BY THE WHITE MAN?
HOW DARE YOU TALK LIKE THAT ABOUT OUR SAVIOR!
HUEY: GOD I LOVE YOU .. UNFORTUNATLEY OUT OF MY LEAUGE!
WAY OVER MY HEAD!

ANAND: PAUL HAD TO VETO YOUR REQUEST FOR THE TRANSFER AND LET THAT WASTE PRODUCT GABE HAVE THAT POSITION ..BUT PAUL HAS SOME GOOD NEWS ..
IT'S KIND OF A SECRET BUT YOUR ASSE ENGINEER TITLE DOES HAVE A SCALE AND BECAUSE YOU'LL BE STAYING WITH US HERE IN DESIGN I AM GOING TO FILE THE PAPERS TO UP YOUR PAY TO THE MAX
YOU SHOULD SEE THE CHANGE IN THE SECOND PAY CHECK AFTER THE NEXT
THANKS PAUL: AND I WILL KEEP IT TO MYSELF -SOMETHING MY FELLOW OFFICE MATES HAVE A HARD TIME DOING!

SERIOUSLY MEGHAN...
GOSH: I WOULDN'T EVEN SHARE MY OWN CIRCUMSTANCES! MY DAD IS A BIG SHOT IN CITY GOVERNMENT -I CAME IN AS A MANGER THOUGH MOST OF THESE GUYS CAME IN AS ASSISTANTS FOR LACK OF CONNECTIONS.
I MEAN I'VE BEEN HERE AS LONG AS ANAND - WHAT'S THE DEAL?
I KNEW THIS WAS GOING TO FUCKING HAPPEN! AND TO MAKE THINGS WORSE ANAND'S WIFE IS RELATED TO THE CHIEF!
A LITTLE BIRD IN OUR UNION TOLD ME ANAND IS GETTING A SLIGHT RISE FOR NOT TAKING THAT FIELD POSITION
!!!
WELL: THIS JOB DOES ENABLE ME TO DO MY AMWAY BUSINESS... GIL LOOKS THE OTHER WAY
WELL: I REACH RETIREMENT IN 3 YEARS... I DON'T CARE
FELIX: THAT ANAND JOINED A YEAR AFTER YOU DID -AND HE MAY BE GOOD AS AN ENGINEER -BUT WE SEEM TO RUB EACH OTHER IN THE WRONG WAY!

THREE MONTHS AFTER THE WEDDING ROOPA IS GIVEN HER PR VISA BY THE US CONSULATE IN HYDERABAD - AND ON DECEMBER 7TH, 1991 - IS ON THE LAST LEG OF THE JOURNEY BETWEEN VIZAG AND NEW YORK ...
!!!
RATHER PRETTY ISN'T IT?
HEY - WE STILL HAVE ANOTHER 2 HOURS BEFORE WE LAND IN JFK - COULD WE CHAT? IF IT'S OKAY - I'LL OCCUPY THE VACANT SEAT BETWEEN US ...
HI -I'M PROTIMA - PROTIMA NARAYANA ...
WHY SURE ...

THIS FLYING STUFF IS IN MY BLOOD ... MY LATE DAD WAS A NAVIGATOR IN THE IAF
ACTUALLY - I NEVER STEPPED INTO A PLANE UNTIL NOW ... MY LATE DAD WAS AN ENGINEER FOR THE GOVERNMENT - WE GOT FREE TICKETS FOR RAIL TRAVEL ... SO THE NEED WAS JUST NOT THERE ...
THIS IS CAPTAIN MURTHY - WE WILL BE STARTING OUR DESCENT INTO NEW YORK JFK IN APPROXIMATELY 30 MINUTES ...
I BOUGHT A BOOK TO READ - BUT JUST CAN'T GET MY ATTENTION OFF THE VIEW OUTSIDE THE WINDOW - FOR THE PAST 14 HOURS!
IT'S ABOUT 5 DEGREES CELSIUS IN NEW YORK ..A SLIGHT CHILL ALONG WITH LIGHT PRECIPITATION ,,,
HEY - I THINK THE CAPTAIN MAY HAVE BEEN A AN OLD FRIEND OF MY LATE DAD - I AM GOING TO TRY TO TALK TO HIM IN THE COCKPIT ...

PROTIMA RECOGNIZES THE NAME OF THE CAPTAIN OF THE NEW YORK JFK BOUND BOEING 737 FROM THE INITIAL FLIGHT ANNOUNCEMENT: CAPTAIN MURTHY WAS A PILOT IN THE IAF PRIOR TO JOINING AIR INDIA -AND WAS A COLLEAGUE OF PROTIMA'S LATE FATHER WING COMMANDER NARAYNA
???
CAPTAIN MURTHY?
MY NAME IS PROTIMA - PROTIMA NARAYANA - I THINK YOU WERE THE COLLEAGUE OF LATE FATHER - WING COMMANDER NARAYANA OF THE IAF

YES! DAUGHTER OF MY FRIEND AND NAVIGATOR NARAYAN! I USED TO CALL HIM "NAR" AS A NICKNAME!
WE FLEW MANY A MISSION TOGETHER! IN FACT ONE STORY COMES TO MIND I SIMPLY CAN NOT FORGET ...

NAR : DO YOU SEE WHAT I SEE?
JUNE 1982:
NEAR THE INDO-PAK BORDER - CAPT. MURTHY AND WC NARAYANA ARE ON ROUTINE PATROL. CAPTAIN MURTHY PILOTING A IAF TEJAS - NARAYANA "NAR" THE NAVIGATOR
YES CAPTAIN MURTHY - WHAT THE HELL? IN OUR AIRSPACE !
WITHIN A MINUTE'S TIME - CAPTAIN MURTHY IS FORCED TO REACT ...

CAPTAIN MURTHY - AFTER A MINUTE OF "CAT & MOUSE" - MAKES A DECISION ...
I'M GOING TO TRY AND SCARE THEM ...
GOSH CAPTAIN MURTHY - THAT WAS INDEED A CLOSE CALL! BUT MY DAD NEVER MENTIONED THIS WHEN HE CAME HOME THAT DAY
BAAAAAM
COULDN'T - AT THE TIME EVEN I COULDN'T MENTION IT TO ANYONE OUTSIDE THE IAF

YES CAPTAIN MURTHY - HE ALWAYS SPOKE VERY HIGHLY OF YOU ..
BUT HE NEVER SHARED ANY OF HIS IAF STORIES WITH US WHEN WE WERE SMALL
YES - EVEN I NEVER SHARED ANY OF THESE STORIES WITH MY OWN CHILDREN - WHO ARE NOW ABOUT THE SAME AGE AS YOU ... THOSE DAYS WERE DIFFERENT IN SO MANY WAYS ...
IN ANY CASE - IT WAS WONDERFUL MEETING SOMEONE WHO WAS INDEED CLOSE TO MY FATHER ...

THE PLANE STARTS ITS DESCENT INTO NEW YORK'S JFK AIRPORT
I AM SINGLE - AND WILL REMAIN SO ... NO MAN HAS EVER IMPRESSED ME - CALL IT A BIOLOGICAL THING
WHEN I WAS A TEEN - I OFTEN EXPERIENCED AN ATTRACTION TOWARDS OTHER GIRLS MY AGE ... BUT I THINK IT WAS FOR THE FACT THAT CONVENT SCHOOL I ATTENDED IN BOMBAY WAS NOT COED
WE ARE ONLY A HALF HOUR FROM LITERALLY ANOTHER WORLD .. MY ISSUE WITH MEN WOULD NOT BE A MAJOR ISSUE IN AMERICA .. IF YOU CATCH MY DRIFT

AI FLIGHT 7821 MAKES ITS FINAL DESCENT INTO NEW YORK'S JFK AIRPORT ON THE MORNING OF DECEMBER 8TH, 1991 AT AROUND 6 AM EST...
...PLEASE FASTEN YOUR SEAT BELTS AND OBSERVE THE NO SMOKING SIGNS AND EXTINGUISH ALL CIGARETTES...
ROOPA AND PROTIMA ARE TEMPORARILY SEPARATED IN THE IMMIGRATION QUEUE ...
Please Wait Behind Line 15
Kiosk
UTTER HELL YAAR! AND THIS IS AMERICA!
I'M ACTUALLY ALREADY LIKING IT !
HEY THANKS FOR OFFERING ME A RIDE INTO THE CITY - AS I SAID: MY HOSTEL AT NYU IS JUST A FEW BLOCKS FROM YOUR PLACE ...
B28

ANAND - THIS IS MY NEW FRIEND PROTIMA - SHE'S A PHD STUDENT AT ENTRAL UNIVERSITY IN DERABAD - SHE'S HERE TO GIVE A KUCHIPUDI DANCE WORKSHOP AT YU TISCH ... I AGREED TO LET HER SHARE THE TAXI WITH US
YOUR DORM IS ON WAVERLY PLACE CLOSE TO OUR BUILDING
WE'LL FIRST GET OFF AT MY PLACE - I WILL GIVE THE DRIVER EXTRA TO CONTINUE ON TO YOUR HOSTEL ...
TAXI
HEY GUYS - I EALLY APPRECIATE IS - THEY REALLY 'T REIMBURSE MUCH AND I TRY TO SAVE HATEVER I CAN ON THESE FOREIGN TOURS
HOW LONG DO YOU EXPECT TO BE HERE MA'AM? YOU KNOW - WHEN I WAS YOUNGER I ALWAYS DREAMED OF ATTENDING THE NYU TISCH FILM SCHOOL AND BECOMING ANOTHER SPIKE LEE!
THE WORKSHOP CONCLUDES AT THE END JANUARY - IN TIME FOR THE BEGINNING OF THE SPRING REGULAR SEMESTER AT TISCH - THERE WILL BE A RECITAL AT THE END WHICH YOU BOTH MUST ATTEND ...

IN FRONT OF ANAND'S COOP BUILDING AT 180 THOMPSON STREET IN THE WEST VILLAGE
I SINCERELY THANK YOU ROOPA - YOU SAVED ME ALMOST $50! ENOUGH FOR A MEAL AT A 5 STAR HOTEL IN HYDERABAD!
I'M JUST A 10 MINUTE WALK FROM HERE - SO WE'LL MEET OFTEN DURING THE TIME I'M IN NEW YORK ... I AM GETTING A LOCAL CELL AND WILL CALL YOU AS SOON AS I GET IT ...
YEAH - IT WILL BE NICE TO HAVE SOMEONE CLOSE BY TO VISIT ... ANAND IS AT THE OFFICE SOMETIMES 9 HOURS - AND MY MFA COURSE DOESN'T BEGIN UNTIL FEBRUARY ...

YEAR AFTER ROOPA'S ARRIVAL IN MANHATTAN - SHE HAS BEGUN HER HER FINAL THESIS SEMESTER AT PRATT INSTITUTE'S MFA PHOTOGRAPHY PROGRAM AT ITS CLINTON HILL, BROOKLYN, NY CAMPUS
YOU KNOW ROOPA - WHEN I WAS RAHGGED IN MY FIRST YEAR AT JJ COLLEGE IN BOMBAY - THEY MADE ME ENTER THE GIRL'S HOSTEL DRESSED LIKE THIS ...
I FOUND OUT LATER - SOME OF THE GIRLS WERE ACTUALLY "TURNED ON"
LOOK MISTER SUNIL GANSHANI FROM NAPEAN SEA ROAD WHO IS ABLE TO AFFORD THIS RIDICULOUS TUITION AND BOARD WITHOUT FINANCDIAL AID ...
YOU'RE THE ONE WHO PITCHED THIS IDEA TO THE PROF : THE EVIL FUR INDUSTRY - AND I STILL DON'T UNDERSTAND HOW YOU'RE GOING TO CUT AND PASTE A MINK COAT ONTO YOUR BODY!
OKAY I'LL TAKE DIFFERENT ANGLES FOR YOU TO COMP IN PHOTOSHOP - BUT THE DISTANCE BETWEEN THE CAMERA AND YOU WILL BE FIXED ...
AND REMEMBER - MY HUSBAND DOES NOT LIKE THE SMELL OF OLD SPICE ON ME ...

WE CAN CHECK OUT THE PI SHOP TO SEE IF WE CAN GET SOME COFFEE - I GOT A 1 HOUR COMMUTE ON THE BUS - DON'T TRUST TAKING THE SUBWAY ALONE AT THIS TIME ...
I'LL DOWNLOAD THE IMAGES AND FILE TRANSFER THEM TO YOU TOMORROW MORNING - JUST TOO TIRED TONIGHT ...
LOOKS LIKE IT'S CLOSED - TOO LATE AT NIGHT ON A WEEKEND ...

BEHIND THE ENGINEERING BUILDING .. AWAY FROM THE EYES OF CAMPUS SECURITY ...
I SCORED THIS WEED FROM BENSONHURST BROOKLYN THROUGH MY ITALIAN AMERICAN M ARCH STUDENT ROOMMATE IN THE DORM - AT LEAST HE'S AROUND WEEKDAYS WHEN HE'S NOT AT HOME IN BENSONHURST!
(COUGH COUGH COUGH !) HAI BHAGWAN! THIS IS STRONG STUFF! MUCH STRONGER THAN ANYTHING WE GOT WHEN I WAS A STUDENT IN BOMBAY!
LISTEN - BETTER YOU COME TO MY DORM ROOM FOR THE COFFEE BEFORE YOU LEAVE FOR THE CITY - MY ROOMMATE ALWAYS HAS A POT GOING ...AND THE BATHROOMS ARE CLEANED AND DETAILED EVERY OTHER DAY BY NONE OTHER ...

WALKING ACROSS WILLOUGHBY TO THE DORM ...
THAT'S THE BENEFIT OF LIVING ON CAMPUS - A 4 MINUTE COMMUTE ...
THE NEXT MORNING AT 5 AM
DAMN - WHAT'S THE TIME?
YEAH ... YOU LITERALLY COLLAPSED WHEN YOU GOT HERE YESTERDAY LATE .. MUST HAVE BEEN THAT STRONG WEED ... AND SIMPLE FATIGUE ...
I FOUND YOUR ADDRESS BOOK - AND CALLED YOUR HUSBAND AND TOLD HIM YOU WERE WORKING LATE AND WOULD STAY ON CAMPUS WITH A FRIEND ... GUESS THAT WAS ME!

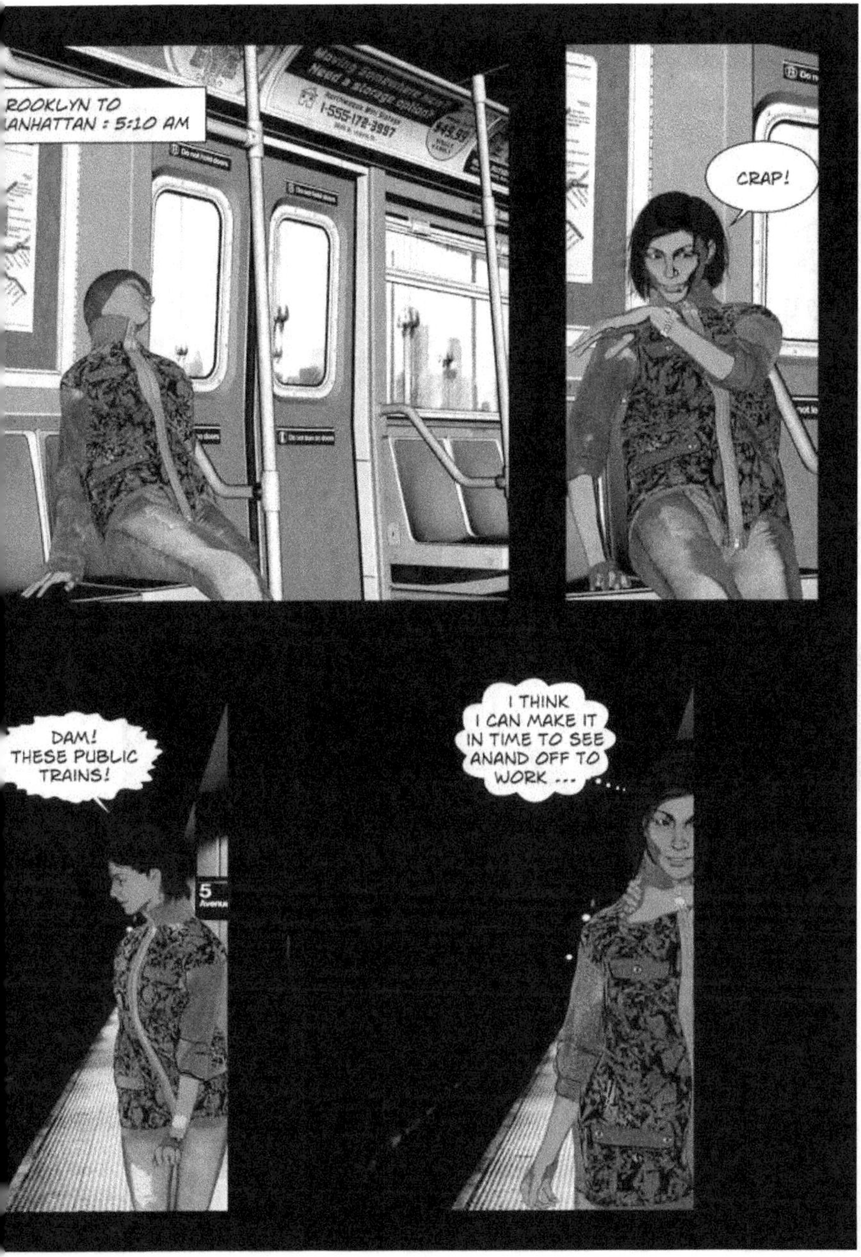

ROOKLYN TO
ANHATTAN : 5:10 AM

CRAP!

DAM!
THESE PUBLIC
TRAINS!

ON THE WAY BACK TO THE APARTMENT FROM BROOKLYN ... WITH THE SMELL OF SUNIL'S COLOGNE ON HER CLOTHES ...
GOD I HOPE I CAN GET HOME BEFORE ANAND GETS UP ...
I MEAN - I DID NOTHING WITH SUNIL - BUT HOW DO I EXPLAIN MY ABSENCE? SUNIL HAS TO HAVE A GENDER CHANGE: SUNITA PERHAPS ..
5 Avenue

West 4 Street-Washington
Square Station
I HAVE A FEELING I MAY HAVE MISSED HIM ...
LO AND BEHOLD : I MISSED HIM!
180 THOMPSON : 5:45 AM
AND THOSE ROACHES - THE COOP BOARD PROMISED TO SEND THE EXTERMINATOR TOMORROW - SO WE HAVE TO REMAIN OUTSIDE THE FLAT FOR 24 HOURS IN THE AFTERMATH ... ANAND'S FRIEND PRINNY OFFERED TO HOST US FOR THE NIGHT ... SWEET GIRL ...

KNOCK KNOCK !!!
JUST A SECOND SUNIL ...
THANKS FOR BUZZING ME IN ... AND THANK GOD NO DOORMAN TO SPY ON THIS VISIT ... YOU LEFT YOUR PURSE IN MY DORM ROOM - I AM ASSUMING YOUR HUSBAND IS AT WORK NOW
WELL - YOU MIGHT AS WELL COME IN - IT'S LITERALLY FREEZING IN THAT HALLWAY ...
NICE PHOTO! BUT WHERE'S THE 'BETTER HALF'?
TAKING THE PIC OF COURSE! BACK THEN - I HAD NO CLUE AS TO HOW THAT HIS NIKON F3 WORKED! NOW THAT I HAVE MADE PHOTO TAKING MY FUTURE OCCUPATIO ... THERE IS RUMOR IN THE INDUSTRY THAT 'DIGITAL' WILL SOMEDAY TAKE OVER FILM ..I'M DOOMED BEFORE I EVEN START!

C'EST ICI ! MA CHÈRE ROOPA - BONNE MERDE! I SPENT 5 YEARS LEARNING FRENCH FROM THOSE CREEPY NUNS IN THAT BOMBAY CONVENT - WHEN NOT SMOKING WEED IN THE CONFESSION STALL - IT PAYS OFF IN TIMES LIKE THIS!
THE REASON I REQUESTED YOU TO COME OUTDOORS ONTO THE BALCONY - YOUR HUSBAND WOULD HAVE A LITERAL BOVINE (COW) IF HE GOT A WHIFF OF THIS SHIT
NOT THE SHIT ITSELF - ITS SOURCE ...ME
COUGH ! COUGH !
SUNIL: TAKE IT EASY!

ON THE WAY BACK TO THE PRATT CAMPUS AFTER RETURNING ROOPA'S PURSE ...
TO BE ...
... OR NOT "DOOBEE"
WHY NOT? EVERYONE ELSE SEEMS TO BE DOING IT !

???
!!!
HEY DUDE - LOOKS LIKE YOU'VE GOT SOME GOOD SHIT THERE !
YOU GOT ANYTHING FOR SALE?

NO MAN - I DON'T SELL - THIS WAS THE LAST OF WHAT I HAD - I AM NO ADDICT ... NOR A DEALER ...
OKAY - GOT IT - I AM NO ORDINARY BUYER EITHER ...
!!!
LISTEN - I CAN TELL BY YOUR ACCENT - ARE YOU PAKISTANI ?

OFFICER - I AM BEGGING YOU - IF YOU ARREST ME I WILL NOT BE ABLE TO BE A STUDENT IN YOUR COUNTRY ...
NOW YOU REALIZE THAT PAL?
PLEASE OFFICER - I BEG YOU - THIS ISN'T SOMETHING I DO AS A HABIT !
LISTEN : I DO HAVE A HEART - I'M GOING TO LET YOU GO IN THIS CASE ...
SO UNLESS YOU WISH TO GO BACK TO BOMBAY AFTER A STAY IN JAIL ... YOU BETTER THINK ABOUT THIS BEFORE YOU TRY THIS AGAIN !

OKAY FOLKS - THE COAST IS CLEAR -HAVE A PRODUCTIVE MEETING -AND ANAND: BELIEVE!
DR PA McCABE PE PhD DIRECTOR COMM ENGINEERING
ANAND: WHAT THE F**CK IS GOING ON WITH YOU? EVERY SINCE YOUR WIFE JOINED YOU HERE FROM INDIA -YOUR BEHAVIOR - DARESAY 'ATTITUDE' -HAS GONE HAYWIRE!
I SPECIFICALLY TOLD YOU ON THAT TRIP WE TOOK TOGETHER LAST SUMMER TO JONES BEACH - WHEN YOU HAVE A GOOD THING GOING: KEEP IT TO YOURSELF!
OUR EAP -EMPLOYMENT ASSISTANCE PEOPLE - HAVE BEEN CONTACTED TO GET YOU HELP FROM WHATEVER IT IS THAT'S BOTHERING YOU
MEGHAN -YOU DON'T HAVE ANY IDEA WHAT LITERAL HELL I'M GOING THROUGH EVER SICNE THAT WOMAN ARRIVED

PRINNY MEETS ANAND AFTER WORK EVERY OTHER DAY TO EXERCISE - AN EXCUSE FOR PRINNY TO HANG OUT WITH HER PAST LOVER ...
NO WORRIES DUDE - AS LONG AS PRINNY IS HERE - YOU HAVE NOTHING TO FEAR ..
AND THE SAME FOR THAT MAIL ORDER BRIDE - ONCE SHE GETS HER GREENCARD OR WHATEVER - HE'LL NEVER KNOW WHAT SHE'S GONNA DO NEXT ...

WELL WELL ANAND - I GET THE JIST: YOU'RE PUMPING UP FOR THE BRIDE!
JUST TWO MORE REPS ANAND ! C'MON I KNOW YOU CAN DO IT DO IT FOR THAT MAIL ORDER BRIDE THAT'S DUE TO POP IN AT ANY MOMENT !
IF YOU REALLY WANNA IMPRESS YOUR FUCK BUDDY PRINNY - ANOTHER TWO SETS !

GOING BACK DOWNTOWN ON THE D TRAIN AFTER THE MIDTOWN GYM : PRINNY USED HER CONTACTS TO GET ANAND A DISCOUNTED MEMBERSHIP
YOU BASTARD - I WANTED A CHILD BY YOU - NOW YOU THROW YOUR MAIL ORDER INDIAN BRIDE INTO MY FACE ... FUCK YOU !
LIKE THAT SONG BY LED ZEPPELIN: "DON'T IT MAKE YOU WONDER?"

DUDE: AREN'T YOU A LONG WAY FROM BROOKLYN?
SUNIL: GET IT THROUGH YOUR HEAD -WE ARE JUST PLATONIC FRIENDS -ANYTHING ELSE ...WELL ...IS JUST PLAIN EVIL !
I AM INDEED A FOOL -BUT I HEARD GOD LIKES FOOLS

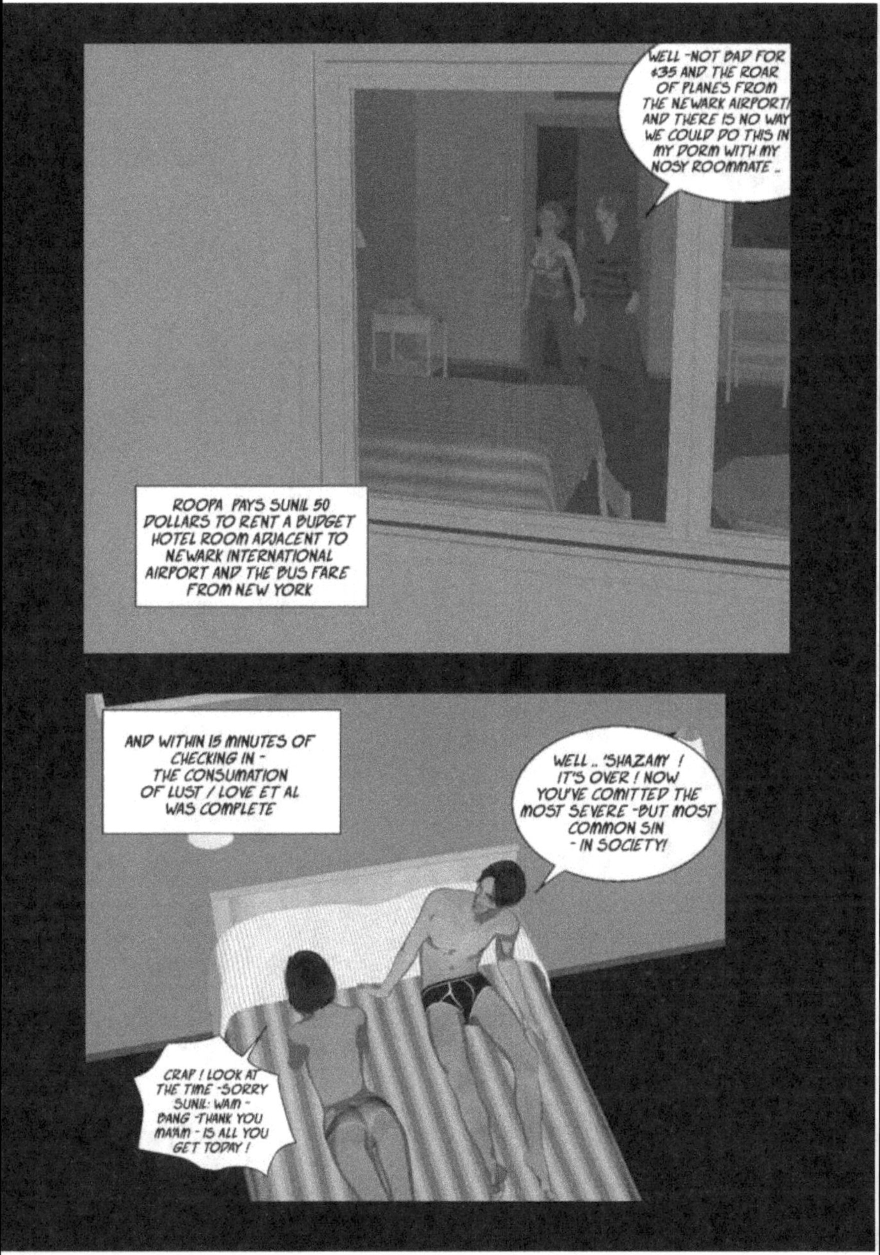

WELL -NOT BAD FOR $35 AND THE ROAR OF PLANES FROM THE NEWARK AIRPORT AND THERE IS NO WAY WE COULD DO THIS IN MY DORM WITH MY NOSY ROOMMATE ..

ROOPA PAYS SUNIL 50 DOLLARS TO RENT A BUDGET HOTEL ROOM ADJACENT TO NEWARK INTERNATIONAL AIRPORT AND THE BUS FARE FROM NEW YORK

MY MY MY: WHAT A MESS YOU'RE BOTH IN! ROOPA WANTS TO "KEEP THE BABY" AS PER THE POP TUNE BY MADONNA -AND ANAND WISHES TO HAVE NO PART IN THE CHILD ..
FYI: ANAND IS NOT A VERY "SEXUAL" PERSON: IN THE FEW TIMES WE "DID IT" HE ALWAYS WORE PROTECTION
I MEAN ROOPA: ARE YOU POSITIVE IT'S MINE? SHOULDN'T WE DO A PATERNITY TEST BEFORE GOING INTO PANIC MODE?
IN ANY CASE: I DON'T WISH ANAND TO KNOW ABOUT THIS -I DO IN FACT STILL LOVE HIM AND THIS WOULD BE THE WORST THING ANY WIFE COULD DO TO HER HUSBAND
DAMN DAMN DAMN! THERE IS NO BENEVOLENT GOD!
GOD! THIS MAY BE A GOOD OPPORTUNITY FOR ME TO HAVE ROOPA LIVE WITH ME IN HYDERABAD - BEING "GAY" IN HYDERABAD IS NOT AS EASY AS HERE IN THE STATES: BUT ASKING HER IS A RISK: ALL THAT CATHOLIC STUFF! SHE MAY LITERALLY FREAK!

ROOPA INTRODUCES SUNIL TO THE 92ND "Y" - WHICH SHE DISCOVERED THROUGH HER FRIEND PROTIMA, WHO GAVE A KUCHIPUDI DEMO HERE PRIOR TO HER RETURN TO HYDERABAD
AIKIDO IS DIFFERENT FROM THAT TAE KWON DO YOU LEARNED IN MUMBAI ...
WHILE WE WAIT FOR CLASS TO START - I'LL SHOW YOU THE BASICS OF TAKING A FALL
NOW - AS I HAD SHOWN YOU BEFORE ...
ROOPA!!!

AT THE 92ND STREET Y ...ROOPA IS IN THE FIRST TRIMESTER OF HER CARRYING SUNIL'S CHILD
I THOUGH (AND THOUGHT) WHAT TO DO ...
!!??
SUNIL: I CAN'T HAVE AN ABORTION - IT'S AGAINST EVERYTHING I BELIEVE IN
I'VE DECIDED TO LEAVE ANAND - AND YOU - TO RETURN TO INDIA TO HAVE THE CHILD ...

GIVEN YOU'RE UNWILLING TO GET AN ABORTION - AND IT'S APPARENT THAT IT'S NOT ANAND'S - WHAT OTHER CHOICE ARE YOU LEFT WITH?
AND THAT'S WHATS REALLY THE MOST HORRID ASPECT : ANAND - IN THE PAST 3 YEARS OF OUR MARRAIGE - NEVER HARMED ME IN ANY WAY .. THE TUITION FOR MY MFA - EVERYTHING WAS REFLECTIVE OF HIS LOVE
GOD DAMN THOSE NUNS AT THAT CONVENT SCHOOL BACK HOME!
LISTEN: I LEAVE BACK FOR HYDERABAD IN A FEW DAYS - I SUGGEST YOU COME BACK TO INDIA WITH ME AND HAVE YOUR CHILD THERE ..YOU'RE ALWAYS WELCOME AT MY PLACE - I LIVE ALONE AND COULD BENEFIT FROM HAVING AN EDUCATED ROOMMATE
REMEMBER WHO YOU ARE TALKING TO ! I AM NOW FACULTY AT HYDERABAD CENTRAL WITH YOUR MFA FROM A FAMOUS NEW YORK INSTITUTE - THERE WOULDN'T BE ANY OBSTACLES FOR YOU TO GET A FACULTY POSITION EITHER AT MY PLACE OR JNTU

SUNIL - AT THIS POINT IT'S NOT A QUESTION OF "LOVE" RATHER - IT'S THE DU NAY: OBLIGATION BETWEEN A MOTHER AND HER CHILD ...
I AM LEAVING NEW YORK FOR INDIA WITH MY FRIEND PROTIMA TOMORROW MORNING
AND SUNIL: PLEASE DON'T FEEL OBLIGATED - I HAVE TO BE TRUTHFUL AND TELL YOU IT WAS ALL LUST ON MY SIDE: THERE IS AND THERE WILL NEVER WILL BE "LOVE" IN OUR RELATIONSHIP - I DON'T WISH TO EVER SEE YOU AGAIN AFTER TODAY ...

ANAND: BY THE TIME YOU WATCH THIS VIDEO - I WOULD ALREADY LEFT FOR INDIA ... THERE IS SIMPLY NO WAY CAN EXPLAIN TO YOU WHAT AN EVIL THING I DID - TO CAUSE THIS DEPARTURE
BUT ANAND - ONE THING IS FOR SURE: DESPITE YOUR DOTING LOVE: I COULD NEVER RETURN YOUR LOVE - AS I HAD BEEN IN LOVE WITH A COLLEGE CLASSMATE AND NEVER REALLY WAS HEALED AFTER HE DUMPED ME FOR A GIRL OF HIS FAMILY'S CHOICE
WAS WHAT I DID TO YOU WRONG? MOST CERTAINLY - I KNEW THIS MIGHT OCCUR - WHICH IS WHY I MADE YOU SIGN THAT AGREEMENT JUST BEFORE OUR WEDDING
AND SINCE YOU DID NOTHING IN TERMS OF HARMING ME - AND EVEN PAID FROM YOUR SAVINGS THE TUITION FOR MY MFA AT PRATT INSTITUTE
ROOPA BEGINS SOBBING - AND THE VIDEO CAMERA IS SHUT OFF: SUNIL GANSHANI THE PERSON OPERATING THE OLD VHS TAPE CAMERA

ANAND !!!
WHAT THE F**K DID YOU DO TO YOURSELF?
PRINNY?
AT LENOX HOSPITAL IN GREENWICH VILLAGE
I KNEW SOMETHING LIKE THIS WAS GOING TO HAPPEN: MAY THAT ROOPA BITCH BURN IN HELL !

WHAT HAPPENED AFTER THEY PUMPED YOUR STOMACH AND PUT CHARCOAL UP YOUR ASS TO GET OUT THAT MED I PRESCRIBED YOU - INSTEAD OF 2 PILLS A DAY - YOU EMPTIED THE ENTIRE BOTTLE OF 100 PILLS INTO YOUR SYSTEM - ANAND ! CMON !
WELL: TO DISAPPOINT YOU - THERE WERE NO VISIONS, LIGHTS AND PEARLY GATES ... JUST (STOPS)
A CARTOON PIG ENGULFED IN ABSOLUTE DARKNESS
DOCTOR: NOTHING .. THEY SHIFTED ME TO THE PSYCH WARD -MY FRIEND PRINNY FINALLY SIGNED ME OUT AMA : AGAINST MEDICAL ADVICE
SO NOTHING - NO VISIONS OF A BETTER EXISTENCE? NO PURGATORY, NO LIMBO: NOTHING ???

GOD DAMN THAT ROOPA BITCH ! MAY SHE BURN IN HER CATHOLIC CONVENT HELL!
I HAVE SOMETHING OF A SIXTH SENSE - I FELT IT COMING ON STRONG WHEN I WAS ON THE TRAIN WITH ANAND ON THE WAY HOME ...
WELL - THANKS TO PRINNY - HE IS ALIVE - BUT IN A COMA ...I TRIED FINDING OUT IF HE HAD AN EMERGENCY CONTACT - HE HAD LISTED PRINNY

HELLO ANAND - I'M DR. CHU - I WORK IN THE PSYCHIATRY DEPARTMENT IN THIS HOSPITAL
GOD ! PLEASE GET THIS CLOWN OUT OF MY FACE !
WE ALMOST LOST YOU THIS MORNING: WHAT COULD HAVE MADE YOU WISH TO HARM YOURSELF LIKE THAT?
WE'RE GOING TO ADMIT YOU INTO THE PSYCH WARD UNTIL WE ARE CONFIDENT YOU WON'T DO THIS TO YOURSELF AGAIN ...

Lenox
THANKS PRINNY - FOR SIGNING ME OUT OF THAT PLACE -I THOUGHT OF ASKING MEGHAN - BUT DECIDED TO KEEP THIS MATTER OUT OF MY OFFICE GOSSIP
1807
ANAND : I HATED THAT BITCH FROM THE MOMENT SHE LANDED IN NEW YORK -I MEAN : WHAT A CUNT ! I REALLY (REALLY) CAN'T UNDERSTAND WHY YOU TIED THE KNOT WITH THAT WOMAN - AND THAT *TOO* AFTER 3 WEEKS OF KNOWING EACH OTHER
KARMA - THAT'S WHAT WE INDIANS CALL IT -GOD WORKS IN STRANGE AND MYSTERIOUS WAYS THEY SAY
(ANAND - GIMME A FUCKING BREAK!)

IT WAS OVER BEFORE IT EVEN STARTED ... THE MAIN REASON SHE MADE ME SIGN THAT PRENUPITAL AGREEMENT WAS SO SHE COULD SPLIT ONCE SHE GOT HER GREENCARD AND MFA
ANAND - ROOPA NEVER CAME OFF TO ME AS A PERSON WHO WOULD DO THAT IN A PREMEDITATED WAY .. WITH SUCH EVIL INTENT ...
AGAIN: I AM NOT A GOOD JUDGE WITH RESPECT TO RELATIONS: AS I HAD SAID MANY TIMES BEFORE YOU BROUGHT ROOPA TO THE STATES - I WOULD GLADLY HAVE HAD YOU AS MY SPOUSE ... NOW: PLEASE (PLEASE) DON'T DO ANYTHING STUPID!

HELLO? ANAND RAO JI? THIS IS ZAREENA ... I WAS THE FLIGHT ATTENDANT ON THAT BOMBAY TO JFK AIR INDIA FLIGHT ..
ZAREENA! ALWAYS THE 'GO GETTER'!
HELLO ..YES. THIS IS ANAND ...ZAREENA? I DON'T RECALL ..
OKAY ...OKAY ...GOT THE IDEA. I'LL MEET UP WITH YOU OUTSIDE THE STORE AFTER I GET OFF OF WORK AROUND 5:45 PM

CONWAY
WE'LL ANAND RAO - YOU'VE FULLFILLED YOUR SIDE OF THE DEAL - LET'S GET A CAB AND WE'LL TRY TO DO OUR FAVOR TO YOU
CONWAY
YEAH "WHY CONWAYS? AND NOT MACYS?" WELL ANAND - THIS GOVERMENT JOB - HOWEVER GLAMOROUS - DOESN'T PAY MUCH
CONWAY
I KNOW IT MUST BE RATHER A LONELY SITUATION - WAITING FOR YOU WIFE TO JOIN YOU HERE ... BUT I TAKE IT YOU'RE A MODERN MAN - WHO IS OPEN MINDED ..
I HOPE YOU DIDN'T GET THE IMPRESSION THAT IT WOULD BE ME OR AISHA WHO WOULD BE ENTERTAINING YOU TONIGHT - I'M TAKING YOU TO A PLACE NEARBYE RUN BY A FORMER FRIEND FROM BOMBAY

SR14
TAKE THE STEPS UPTO THE 3RD FLOOR AND KNOCK ON THE DOOR FOR APARTMENT E1 - MY FRIEND FARAH WILL ANSWER -TELL HER YOU'RE ZAREENA'S FRIEND
WE'RE GOING TO WALK BACK TO OUR HOTEL. YOU'LL BE IN SAFE HANDS : AND DON'T PAY FOR ANYTHING -I'M RETURNING A FAVOR INTRODUCING YOU TO FARAH'S PLACE
GOD! THIS PLACE STINKS OF LIVERWURST AND STALE BEER!
KNOCK! KNOCK! KNOCK!

WELL GALS: A NEWBIE TO OUR CLUB FOR GENTLEMEN - AN ENGINEER ANAND
PLEASE INTRODUCE YOURSELVES
I'M CINDY: I LOVE THE COMPANY OF SUAVE EDUCTATED MEN - WHAT GIRL DOESN'T?
I'M BELINDA : I AM A COLLEGE STUDENT - THIS IS MY SUMMER JOB - I LIKE WHAT I DO

ANAND: I CAN TELL BY YOUR EYES AND BODY LANGUAGE SEEING A SEX WORKER IS SOMETHING OF A NOVELTY -I'M FROM AUSTRALIA WHERE THIS SORT OF BUSINESS IS LEGAL AND QUITE COMMON ..
YOU CAN CHOOSE WHOEVER YOU WISH : BUT I REQUEST YOU CONSIDER THAT I CAN ADDRESS THINGS BEYOND JUST A SUCK AND FUCK
WHEN I WAS A TODDLER LIVING IN THE OUTBACK MY PARENTS DIED IN A AUTO ACCIDENT -AND I WAS SUBSEQUENTLY ADOPTED BY A TRIBE OF AUSTRALIAN NATIVE ABORIGINES AS THEIR OWN..
!!!
IF YOU LET ME A CHANNEL: I CAN TAKE YOU TO A PLACE WITHIN YOUR SUBCONCIOUS MIND THAT YOU HAVE PROBABLY NEVER BEEN

YOU'RE GOING TO ENTER AN ALTERNATE REALITY SHORTLY - JUST REMEMBER, I'M ALWAYS HERE WITH YOU
ANAND RAO OF MANHATTAN NEW YORK : WHAT IS YOUR SINCEREST DESIRE?
IM NOT SURE HOW SAVVY YOU ARE TO OUR HINDU EPISTOMOLOGY: MOKSHAM
AND YOU'RE CORRECT. MY KNOWLEDGE OF YOUR ULTIMATE REALITY IS INDEED LIMITED AS YOUR'S IS OF OURS

ABIGAIL:
I'M OUT OF MY BODY
LOOKING DOWN
AT BOTH OF US -
I AM MOVING RAPIDLY
AWAY IN TIME AND SPACE
RETURNING TO THE EXAVT POINT
IN TIME AND SPACE -TO THE
BROTHEL 2ND AKA AFFAIR
ANAND NOW IS AWARE FOR
SURE THAT ROOPA WILL
INDEED LEAVE - BUT AT
A POINT WHERE SHE USED
HIM THOROUGHY
THE MOMENT WAS BLISS
-LIKE THE KETAMINE
ANASTHESIA HE WAS
GIVEN PRIOR TO HIS
ECT TREATMENT
AFTER ROOPA
LEFT HIM DEVASTATED
SO WHAT CONCLUSIONS,
IF ANY HAVE YOU TO
REGARDING YOUR
YET TO ARRIVE
MAIL ORDER BRIDE
FROM VIZAG??

YOU WALKED ONE EVENING ON THE BEACH OUTSIDE THE RESORT HOTEL
SHE WAS EXCITED ABOUT THE PROSPECT OF A NEW LIFE WITH THE ISSUANCE OF HER VISA PAPERS
HEMANT - WHAT HAVE I DONE !
I ... WAS IN LOVE - SHE WAS WITH SOMEONE BACK IN COLLEGE IN BOMBAY
???
AND DESPITE HER TELLING YOU SO - IN SO MANY WORDS - YOU STILL WENT AHEAD AND MARRIED HER!
AMBITIOUS CLEVER YOU LADY!
KIND WORDS TO DESCRIBE HER ANAND!

9 HOURS AFTER ANAND HAS JOURNEYED AND RETURNED TO EARTH IN AN ALTERNATE TIME SPACE CONTINUUM
HE SHOULD BE OUT OF THE OTHER WORLD ANY MINUTE
AND WHAT AMAZES ME IS THAT YOU DIDN'T GIVE HIM MUCH OF THAT SACRED FLOWER
WHAT? WHERE? HOW?

WILL HE BE OKAY?
DON'T WORRY - HE WILL RETURN AS SOON AS HIS BUSINESS IN THE OTHER WORLD CONCLUDES ...
I SENSE SOMETHING RATHER PROFOUND IS BOTHERING HIM - OTHERWISE HE WOULD BE OUT OF THE OTHER WORLD SOONER ...
ANAND! WAKE UP! IT'S ME ABIGAIL ...

ANAND: WHAT'S GOING ON? I AM AWARE YOUR'RE SOME HOW CONNECTED TO THE BIG GUY UPSTAIRS -AND HE EVEN SIGNED A LETTER OF RECOMMENDATION TO THE NYU MBA PROGRAM -BUT DESPITE ALL THIS GOOD FORTUNE -I'VE ALSO BEEN SEEING A SIGNIFICANT DECREACE IN YOU ABILITY TO DO WORK ON TIME ..
OTHER THINGS LATELY HAVE EVRYONE CONCERNED: COMING INEBRIATED FROM THE LUNCH -SLURRING YOUR VOICE FROM PERHAPS ONE TOO MANY ...I KNOW THAT THERE IS A UNION TO PROTECT YOU ..
...I BELIEVE IN ANAND - AND DON'T WANT YOU TO GO ASTRAY -WITH WHATEVER ISSUES ARE THE SOURCE OF YOUR RELATIVE INCOMPETENCE ...I'VE TELLING YOU EVER SINCE YOU CLEARED THE FE EXAM - GET YOUR PE LICENSE AN MBA HAS NO VALUE HERE !
I WOULD HAVE ASSUMED THAT WIFE OF YOURS WOULD HAVE POPPED OUT CHILREN BY NOW -INSTEAD OF LEAVING YOU HIGH AND DRY WITH LITTLE EXPLANTION. AGAIN: THIS IS NONE OF BUSINESS - BUT ALWAYS UNDERSTAND THAT I AM ON YOUR SIDE: OUR MOST BRILLIANT YOUNG ENGINEER ..
I TOOK THAT LIBERTY OF HAVING MEGHAN CHOY - I KNOW YOU'RE BOTH ARE FRIENDS IN ADDITION TO WORK MATES -FOR YOU TO SEE A COUNSELER THROUGH THE CITY'S EAP PROGRAM ...PLEASE DO TAKE ADVANTAGE OF THIS BENEFIT - I SIMPLY CAN'T STAND TO WITNESS YOU FALL INTO PIECES AND ULTIMATELY LEAVE NOT BECAUSE OF YOUR CHOICE

AND THE TRAGI-COMEDY CONTINUES: THE CUCKLOD HUSBAND GETS HIS REVENGE
HENNESS

WELCOME TO HENNESSY'S MATE .. LET ME KNOW IF YOU'LL HAVE ANOTHER PINT

I CAN GUESS YOU'RE A FRIEND OF FARAH'S UPSTAIRS .. WE ALWAYS OFFER A FREE FIRST PINT TO HER CLIENTS
YOU MEAN YOU KNOW WHAT GOES ON -ON THE 3RD FLOOR?

YEAH -WELL: IT'S A RATHER COMPLICATED BUSINESS RELATIONSHIP - WE LOOK THE OTHER WAY - AND INFORM HER IF AN UNDERCOVER NYPD IS CASING THE JOINT -SHE GIVES A MONTHLY PAYCHECK IF YOU KNOW WHAT I MEAN

HI ANAND - WELCOME BACK !
YES - I CAME TO SEE ABIGAIL - THAT AUSTRALIAN GIRL
OH - ABIGAIL - SHE LEFT THE COUNTRY BACK TO AUSTRALIA - SOME KIND OF FAMILY ISSUE
BELINDA IS HERE THOUGH - SHE COULD GIVE YOU A GOOD TIME FOR YOUR MONEY ...
SURE - WHY NOT? MONEY IS MONEY ...

DARK MEAT: BUT NOT BAD ON THE EYES !
YOUR LAST VISIT WAS TAKEN CARE OF BY MY EX COLLEAUGE AT AIR INDIA AND FRIEND ZAREENA --BUT THIS TIME YOU NEED TO DONATE $300 TO OUR CLUB FOR A 1 HOUR VISIT ...
BELIEVE IT OR NOT - I AM A 3RD YEAR STUDENT AT VASSAR IN POUGHKEEPSIE - I'M A PSYCHOLOGY MAJOR - THIS IS HOW I PAY IN PART FOR MY TUITION - THOUGH MY PARENTS ARE AFFLUENT ENOUGH TO ALLOW ME TO BE FREE EVERY SUMMER ...BUT AS I SAID: I LOVE WHAT I DO - AND FARAH KEEPS OUT THE UGLY GUYS SO WE DON'T HAVE TO FAKE IT
WHAT DO I DO FOR FUN ? - YOU'RE EXPERIENCING IT !

ANAND - I HAVE SOME GOOD NEWS : YOU ARE GOING TO BE ELIGIBLE FOR BOTH WORKMAN'S COMP AND LONG TERM DISABILITY : YOU HAVE PAUL TO THANK FOR PULLING THE STRINGS WITH HIS CONTACT IN NEW YORK STATE AND THE FEDS ..
YES I UNDERSTAND THAT WOMAN LEFT YOU HIGH AND DRY: YOU SPENDING YOUR SAVINGS ON HER MFA COURSE
I DREAM YOU'LL MARRY ME AFTER FINALLY GETTING A DIVORCE FROM THAT BITCH - I GUESS I SHOULD JUST KEEP DREAMING!
BUT ANAND: I'VE GIVEN UP WAITING FOR YOU - I ACCEPTEDA MARRAIGE PROPOSAL FROM A BOY WHO GREW WITH ME HERE IN MANHATTAN'S CHINATOWN ... I HOPE YOU WILL MAKE IT TO OUR WEDDING: WE CHINESE SPEND LAVISHLY ON THE RECEPTION BANQUET !

IT'S 1993 – TWO YEARS SINCE ANAND HAD DIVORCED FROM ROOPA – AND FINDING HIMSELF UNABLE TO LIVE A COMFORTABLE LIFESTYLE ON HIS DISABILITY INCOME – ANAND DECIDES TO RELOCATE TO INDIA
VOID OF FAMILY IN INDIA – HIS PARENTS BOTH OF WHOM PASSED AWAY WHILE HE WAS IN AMERICA – BY LUCK A SECOND COUSIN WROTE HIM AND OFFERED TO ASSIST HIM TRANSITIONING TO A NEW LIFE IN INDIA
CHOICELESS AWARENESS – WHERE DID I HEAR THAT BEFORE?

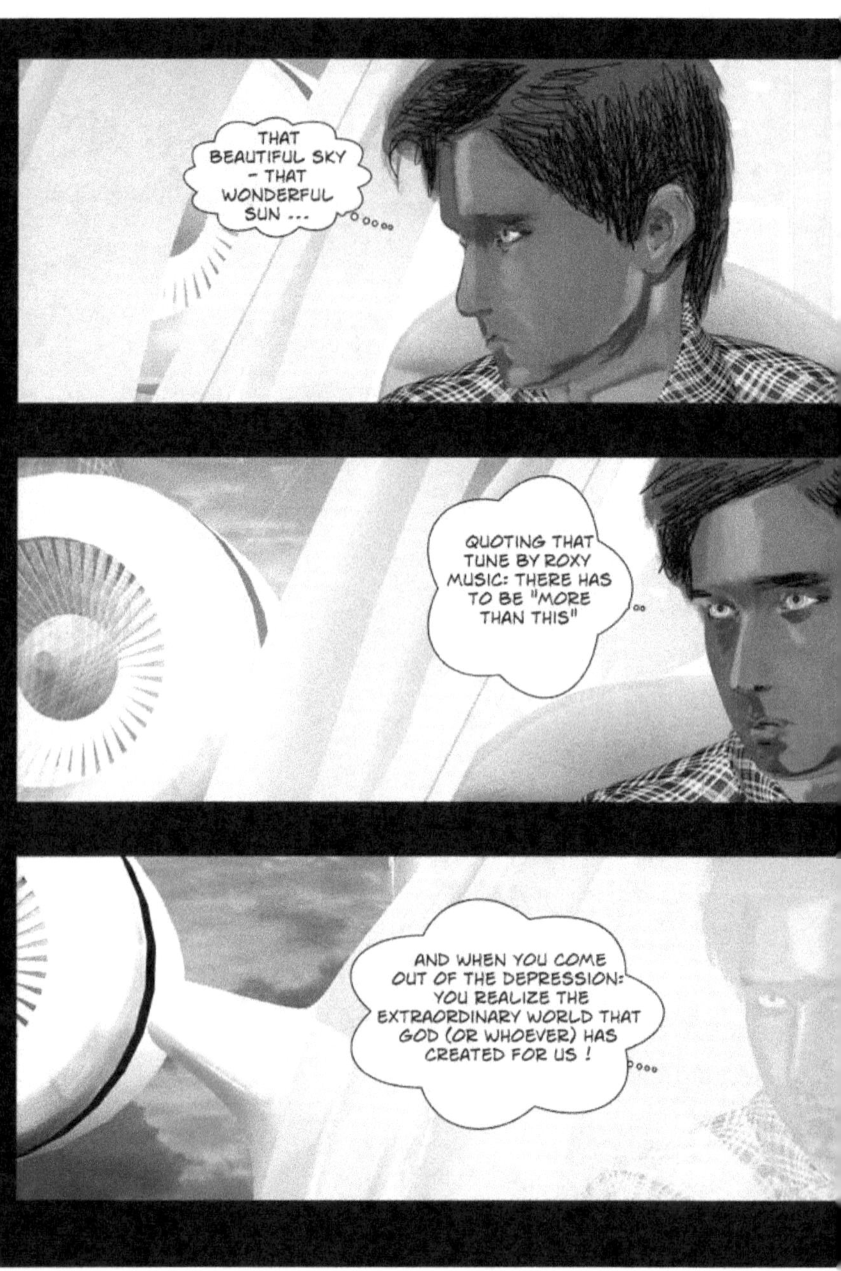
THAT BEAUTIFUL SKY - THAT WONDERFUL SUN ...
QUOTING THAT TUNE BY ROXY MUSIC: THERE HAS TO BE "MORE THAN THIS"
AND WHEN YOU COME OUT OF THE DEPRESSION: YOU REALIZE THE EXTRAORDINARY WORLD THAT GOD (OR WHOEVER) HAS CREATED FOR US !

VISAKHAPATNAM AIRPORT
ANAND RETURNS TO INDIA - FOR GOOD THIS TIME - HIS ONLY RELATIVE IN INDIA - HIS COUSIN ALKA - GREETS HIM IN VIZAG - AND HAS ARRANGED ACCOMMODATIONS FOR HIM - WITHIN HIS BUDGET AFTER TAKING EARLY RETIREMENT
ANAND - OVER HERE !
DID YOU HAVE A GOOD JOURNEY? I MEAN ALL THE WAY FROM NEW YORK TO VIZAG ...

ANAND'S NEW HOME : A ROOM AT THE HARIKA RESORT - OVERLOOKING THE OCEAN AT VIZAG - RUN BY THE AP TOURISM BOARD
I ASSURE YOU: YOU WILL NOT GET ACCOMMODATIONS LIKE THIS FOR THIS PRICE IN YOUR NEW YORK ...
FOR 250 DOLLARS A MONTH - MAYBE A ROOM FOR 3 OR 4 DAYS IN A CHEAP MOTEL IN NEW JERSEY ... THANK GOD I DIDN'T GIVE UP MY INDIAN PASSPORT TO BECOME A NATURALIZED US CITIZEN ..
I THINK VERY HIGHLY OF THE UNITED STATES - BUT SOME SIXTH SENSE TOLD ME THAT ONE DAY I WOULD RETURN TO INDIA PERMANENTLY

AND THE BEST PART: YOU HAVE A ROOM WITH A VIEW !

AND YES: $250 DOLLARS A MONTH - I HAVE TO HAND IT TO ALKA !
YOU PROBABLY NEVER KNEW - BUT WHEN WE WERE KIDS AND OUR FAMILIES WOULD MEET UP AT SOME FUNCTION - I ALWAYS HAD A BAD CRUSH ON YOU - DESPITE THE FACT WE ARE FIRST COUSINS...
CAN I TRUST YOU ANAND? THAT YOU WON'T DO WHAT YOU DID IN NEW YORK?

WOW ! THIS YG FRIEND OF YOURS IS QUITE UPSCALE !
WELL: THIS HOUSE IS OWNED BY ONE OF HIS FOREIGN FRIENDS - AND IS OFFERED TO YG RENT FREE
GOOD EVENING : FRIENDS ALKA AND ANAND - THE OTHERS ARE ALREADY INSIDE

AT YG'S MEETUP - ALKA AND ANAND ARE INTRODUCED ...
PLEASE WELCOME OUR NEW FRIENDS: ALKA AND ANAND
YOU MAY ALREADY HAVE KNOWN : CINDY IS A FORMER FASHION MODEL FROM NEW YORK - THE BABI AN ACTRESS FROM BOMBAY - AND MUKESH BHATT - A PROMINENT FILMMAKER - ALSO FROM BOMBAY

TODAY I WILL BE READING TO YOU ABOUT A TOPIC THAT CONSTANTLY ARISES IN OUR MEETINGS - BY A LATE HERO OF MINE: JIDDU KRISHNAMURTI
AS PER "LOVE" : THE FEELING IS NOT THE DESCRIPTION ; NOT THE WORD - THAT MUCH IS CLEAR ISN'T IT?

AGAIN FRIENDS: IS IT "LOVE" THAT HAS BECOME CLEAR? OR WHAT YOU THINK ABOUT IT?
THE SEEKER STATES : THERE ARE MOMENTS WHEN LOVE SEEMS TO BE ONE THING –BUT AT OTHER MOMENTS IT APPEARS TO BE SOMETHING QUITE DIFFERENT ... ONE DOESN'T KNOW WHERE ONE IS ...

AGAIN: CAN ANY OR ALL OF YOU SEPERATE THE FEELING FOR THE WORD ...AND FROM YOUR PRECONCEPTIONS OF WHAT IT SHOULD OR SHOULD NOT BE?
YES: I'M BEGINNING TO SEE - BUT IN THE PAST WHEN I PROGRAMMED COMPUTERS ...IT WAS ESSENTIAL FOR LABELS TO BE IN PLACE FOR THE PROGRAM TO RUN ...
AND IS THAT FEELING YOU TALK ABOUT - IS IT REAL? OR JUST ANOTHER ONE OF THOSE DELUSIONS I HAVE BEEN DIAGNOSED BY THE SHRINKS IN BOMBAY?
I MAKE MOVIES IN BOMBAY : NONE OF THIS WOULD HOLD WATER GIVEN THE AUDIENCE OF MY FILMS WANTING ENTERTAINMENT - AS OPPOSED TO ENLIGHTENMENT !

ONE CHANCE IN A MILLION - CINDY HARROD RECOGNIZES A "FLING" FROM HER MODELING DAYS IN NEW YORK CITY AT THE PALLADIUM NIGHTCLUB IN MANHATTAN - THE MAN WHO NEVER SHOWED UP FOR A PROMISED DATE ---IN 1986
"SEPERATE" ? I WAS AN ENGINEER IN THE STATES - SO IT WOULD BE HARD - IF NOT IMPOSSIBLE TO SEPERATE THE "FEELING" FROM THE WORD - FROM IT'S DESCRIPTION - FROM THE PERSPECTIVE OF A DIGITAL COMPUTER LETS SAY
ANAND RAO? YOU HAVEN'T CHANGED SINCE WE PARTIED AT THE PALLADIUM IN 1986 - AND NOW MORE THAN 5 YEARS LATER !
AGAIN: APOLOGY - I JUST CAN'T DO IT !

POP
POP
POP
POP
CINDY - YOU'RE DOING GREAT THE CLIENT IS GOING TO LOVE THESE TEST SHOTS
LISTEN CINDY- I KNOW THIS QUESTION IS RATHER UNPROFESSIONAL - BUT THE CLIENT IS VERY INTERESTED IN YOU NOT JUST AS A MODEL FOR HIS PRODUCT .. .DO YOU UNDERSTAND?
WTF ? YOU MEAN THERE'S A CATCH TO GETTING THIS JOB?
LISTEN CINDY- I KNOW THIS QUESTION IS RATHER UNPROFESSIONAL - BUT THE CLIENT IS VERY INTERESTED IN YOU NOT JUST AS A MODEL FOR HIS PRODUCT .. DO YOU UNDERSTAND?
WTF ? YOU MEAN THERE'S A CATCH TO GETTING THIS JOB?

mmmm..
.LOOKS
NICE -WORTH
A TRY
I WOULD LOVE TO
DANCE WITH
YOU: I'M KIND OF
SLOSHED
ON WHITE
RUSSIANS

YEAH: BOOZE ISN'T GOING TO HELP YOU ENJOY - HANGOUT WITH ME TONIGHT ..
I REALLYDON'T HAVE MUCH EXPERIENCE: OUTSIDE SMOKING WEED WITH MY ROOMMATES
WOW: WHAT A CATCH! AND I WILL BE HIS SOURCE OF SUBSTANCE ABUSE!

THIS DUDE IS JUST A KID! HE'S NOT GOING TO GIVE YOU PARTY FAVORS!
I CAN BUY YOU A DRINK -PERHAPS DANCE WITH YOU - BUT I AM JUST A STUDENT - ON A MEASLY GRAD ASSISTANSHIP STRIPEND
SORRY CINDY ... ALL I CAN OFFER YOU IS A WHITE RUSSIAN AND A DANCE

ANAND -IT WASN'T ANYTHING OTHER THAN YOUR ANDROGENOUS GOOD LOOKS THAT ATTRACTED ME -IT WASN'T FOR SOMEONE TO BUY ME BLOW
(SHOUTING) THE KEITH HARING PRINT DROPS TO SIGNIFY THE CLUB WILL CLOSE SHORTLY ...ANAND: WOULD YOU LIKE TO COME TO MY APARTMENT?

THE TUNE "DON'T STOP THE DANCE" BY BRYAN FERRY PLAYS AFTER THE KEITH HARING BACKDROP IS DROPPED – SIGNIFYING THE LAST DANCE BEFORE SHUTTING DOWN FOR THE NIGHT ...
MY PLACE IS IN TRIBECA – BUT I SHARE WITH A ROOMMATE – BUT SHE'S COOL THOUGH WITH HAVING OUR RESPECTIVE GUY DATES TO SLEEP OVER ...
OKAY: BUT TOMORROW IS UNFORTUNATELY A WORKING DAY FOR ME – I TUTOR UNDERGRAD STUDENTS AS PART OF MY GRAD ASSISTANTSHIP – BUT LET'S KEEP IN TOUCH ...MAYBE ON A WEEKDAY?

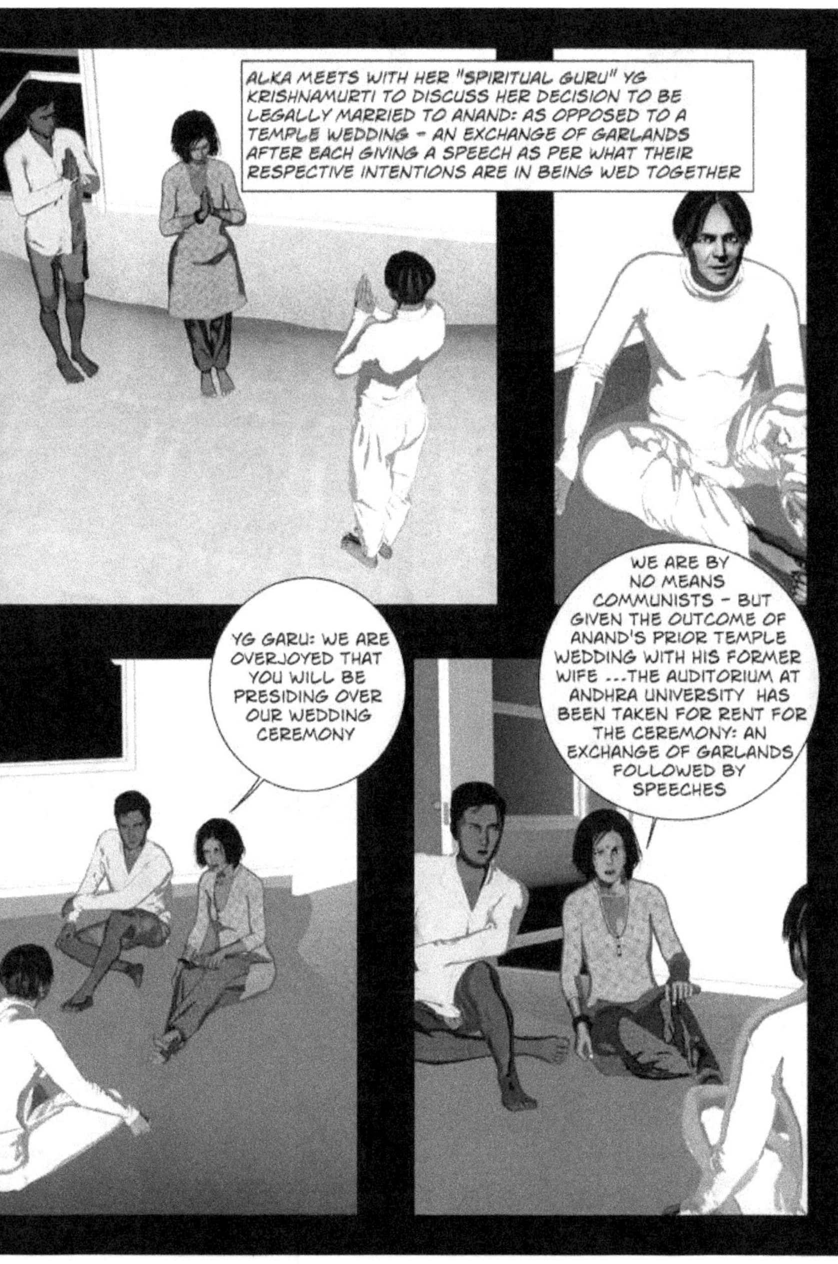
ALKA MEETS WITH HER "SPIRITUAL GURU" YG KRISHNAMURTI TO DISCUSS HER DECISION TO BE LEGALLY MARRIED TO ANAND: AS OPPOSED TO A TEMPLE WEDDING - AN EXCHANGE OF GARLANDS AFTER EACH GIVING A SPEECH AS PER WHAT THEIR RESPECTIVE INTENTIONS ARE IN BEING WED TOGETHER
YG GARU: WE ARE OVERJOYED THAT YOU WILL BE PRESIDING OVER OUR WEDDING CEREMONY
WE ARE BY NO MEANS COMMUNISTS - BUT GIVEN THE OUTCOME OF ANAND'S PRIOR TEMPLE WEDDING WITH HIS FORMER WIFE ...THE AUDITORIUM AT ANDHRA UNIVERSITY HAS BEEN TAKEN FOR RENT FOR THE CEREMONY: AN EXCHANGE OF GARLANDS FOLLOWED BY SPEECHES

C'MON ANAD -
YOU CAN DO IT !
THE BEACH OUTSIDE
YG' HOUSE
THE SILENC
BETWEEN O
WORDS - TH
EBB AND RET
OF THE WAVES
SYNERGY O
NATURE WIT
OUR MORTA
BEINGS
NOW ...
LET'S ENJOY
SILENCE FOR
THE REMAINDER
OF OUR WALK -
SAMHADI IF
POSSIBLE

NAMASTE : TO ALL MY FRIENDS AND FAMILY WHO HAVE COME TO WITNESS THE LAST STEP OF TWO INDIVIDUALS BOND TOGETHER IN A LEGAL UNION
AS MY FRIEND YG GARU WOULD STATE – THE TRADITIONAL INDIAN WEDDING CEREMONY SEEMS SUPERFLUOUS GIVE BOTH I AND ANAND HAD BEEN PREVIOUSLY MARRIED ... BOTH ARRANGED BY OUR RESPECTIVE FAMILIES .. BOTH ENDED FOR LACK OF LOVE ...
NAMASTE ALL: I AM AWARE MOST OF YOU SEATED ARE FROM ALKA'S POOL OF FAMILY AND FRIENDS - I REALLY HAVE NO ONE FROM MY SIDE TO WITNESS THUS CEREMONY...
ALKA AND I BOTH AGREED FOR THIS TYPE OF RITUAL TO BOND US BOTH – AS OF TOMORROW BY FILING FOR AN OFFICIAL MARRIAGE CERTIFICATE

IF THERE IS A GOD - I'M NOT SURE - MAY HE BLESS THIS UNION
ALL I CAN SAY: THANK YOU ALKA - FOR ALLOWING ME A SECOND CHANCE AT LOVE

RAMAKRISHNA BEACH - VIZAG 1994
THE QUESTION : "WHY"?
THE ANSWER: "YES"

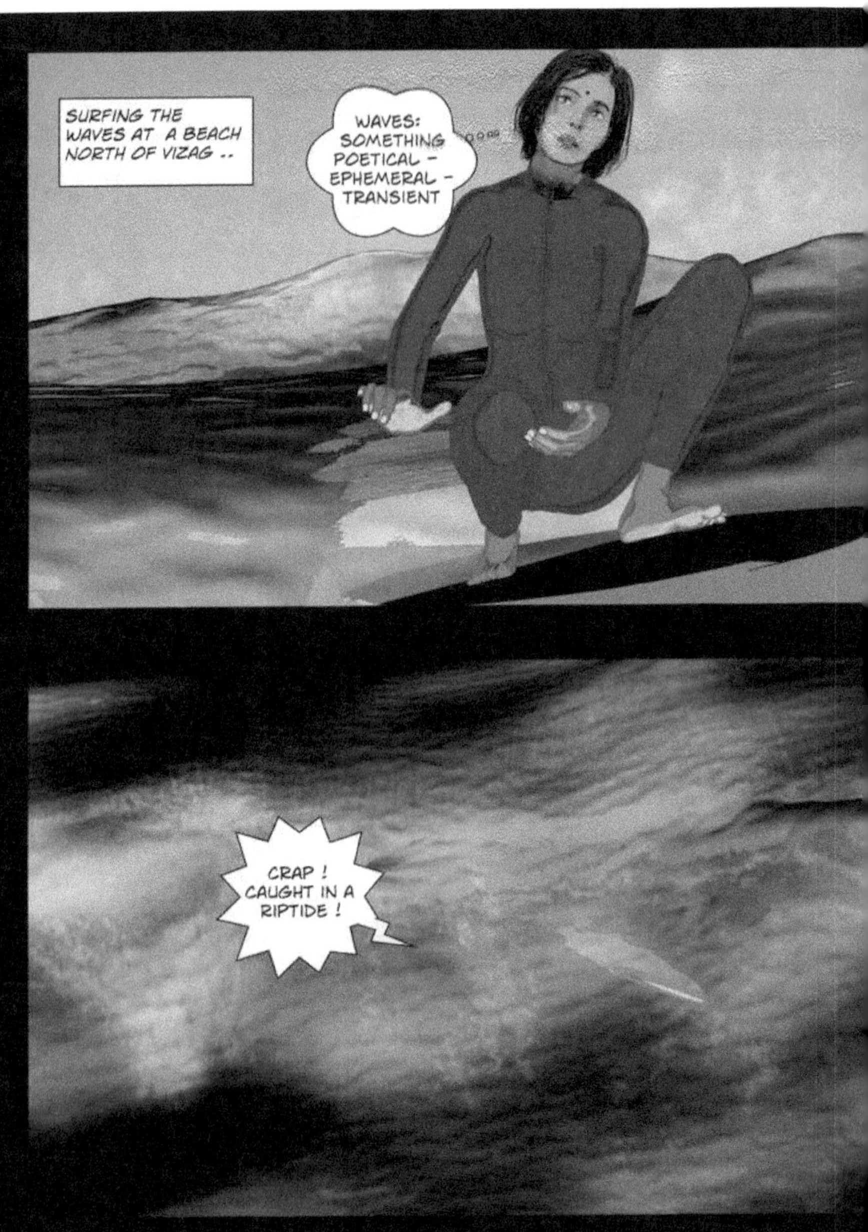
SURFING THE WAVES AT A BEACH NORTH OF VIZAG ..
WAVES: SOMETHING POETICAL - EPHEMERAL - TRANSIENT
CRAP ! CAUGHT IN A RIPTIDE !

WHAT THE
HELL : GOT
CAUGHT IN A
RIPTIDE !
!!!

MA'AM - ARE YOU ALRIGHT NOW? I WAS JUST ABOUT TO CALL AN AMBULANCE BECAUSE YOU WERE OUT FOR MORE THAN 15 MINUTES ...
WOW ! I DON'T EVEN RECALL WHAT HAPPENED - I WAS CAUGHT IN A RIPTIDE THAT SUCKED ME DEEP INTO THE SEA ...

AFTER LIVING IN THE STATES FOR SO MANY YEARS - YOU BEGIN TO APPRECIATE THE BEAUTY OF THE COUNTRY OF OUR ORIGIN - I THOUGHT WE'D TRAVEL LIKE WHEN I WAS A KID - 2ND CLASS ON THE INDIAN RAILWAYS
DO YOU MISS NEW YORK ANAND ? INDIA IS SO DIFFERENT IN SO MANY WAYS ... A FEW YEARS AGO I WAS SENT TO CALIFORNIA FOR SOME IT RELATED WORK - IT'S LIKE COMPARING APPLES AND ORANGES

APPLES AND ORANGES - YES: OF COURSE

AND THE QUETION: AM I AN APPLE OR AN ORANGE ?

IT'S SO COLD IN THE TRAIN - THE WRONG SEASON TO BOOK A/C SLEEPER - YOU CAN'T EVEN OPEN THE WINDOWS

THANK YOU VISIT
JAWAHARLAL NEHRU ZOO PARK, HYDERABAD
NO PARKING
POCKETERS
WAY TO PARKING
THIS PLACE REMINDS ME OF AMERICA - WITH THE WHITE PEOPLE LOOKING AT ME FROM OUTSIDE MY CAGE ...

ENTRANCE:
JAWAHARLAL
NEHRU ZOO PARK,
HYDERABAD INDIA
HOW DO I
KNOW ALKA IS NOT
ANOTHER ROOPA?
WANTING A GREEN CARD
AND A LIFE IN THE
STATES?
I LOVE
ANAND - FOR
SOME REASON HE IS
RATHER SILENT -
QUIET WATER RUNS
DEEP THEY SAY ... AND
HE KNOWS I WENT TO DO
MY TRAINING IN
CALIFORNIA - AND
WASN'T IMPRESSED BY
THE LIVES OF THE
INDIAN IMMIGRANTS
I MET THERE
GOODS NOT ALLOWED IN
Chips Packets
I THINK THE BIKE
RENTAL STALL IS
TOWARDS THE LEFT
OF THE ENTRANCE

WELL - THESE WON'T WIN US A PLACE IN THE TOUR DE FRANCE : THAT'S AN UNDERSTATEMENT!
YOU KNOW - I'VE NEVER REALLY GOTTEN SAD FOR NO REASON ...
SO THIS DEPRESSION: YOU SAY IT MAY HAVE BEEN THERE ALL ALONG - WITH OR WITHOUT THAT ROOPA BITCH ...
I APOLOGIZE: SINCE I AM NOT DEPRESSED FOR NO RHYME OR REASON - I CAN'T REALLY UNDERSTAND WHAT THIS ILLNESS IS ALL ABOUT

ONE THE RETURN TO THEIR HOUSE - A 1 HOUR DRIVE FROM THE ZOO PARK - ALKA REVEALS HER INTENTIONS FINALLY - A TRANSACTION IN TWO CONTEXTS ... ALKA IS BEING TRANSPARENT ...
FACE IT ANAND : IN MANY WAYS THIS IS A MARRIAGE OF CONVENIENCE
WE BOTH NEED EACH OTHER FOR A SUSTAINABLE LIFESTYLE ..
YOUR INCOME MY LOVE; YOUR LOVE - MY INCOME

ON THE WAY TO TANK BUND - FOR AN LATE AFTERNOON WALK
WHERE ARE YOU ANAND? YOU SEEM SO LOST IN YOUR THOUGHTS - YOU BARELY TALK THESE DAYS ...
ALKA: IT'S A RHETORICAL QUESTION FOR WHICH I HAVE NO ANSWER ...

ANAND: WE HAVE A LIMITED TIME ON THIS EARTH IN THIS INCARNATION ... YOU HAVE TO MAKE THE BEST OF IT !
YES: I CONCUR

SO ANAND - YOU ARE NOW FREE OF YOUR OBLIGATIONS TO THE WORLD FOR YOUR SUSTENANCE - I ONLY NEED WORK IF I DESIRE STRUCTURE - AND GET COMPENSATION .. CAN'T *REALLY* BEAT GOD'S BENEVOLENCE !
GOD IN MY OPINION DOES INDEED EXIST - HE WATCHES US FROM A DISTANCE - AND REWARDS OR PUNISHES US BASED ON OUR ACTIONS AND THOUGHTS - I TRULY BELIEVE THIS - NOTHING OCCURS FOR NO REASON ... OR CONVERSELY - EVERYTHING OCCURS FOR A REASON
AMEN !

TANK BAND ROAD
HYDERABAD, INDIA
THE QUESTION: NEVER ASKED HIM
ANAND ...
YES ALKA
WERE YOU SINCERE IN YOUR MOTIVES TO BECOME MY LIFE PARTNER? OR WAS IT SOMETHING IRRATIONAL ?
I DON'T KNOW ALKA - WE WILL HAVE TO WAIT AND SEE ...

TANK BUND-
HYDERABAD
YOU TOLD ME YOUR FIRST WIFE ASKED YOU THIS: "HOW DOES IT FEEL ANAND? NOW BEING A MARRIED MAN?"
UNLIKE THAT WOMAN - I DON'T HAVE A HIDDEN AGENDA - OUTSIDE BEING YOUR LIFE PARTNER TILL DEATH DO US PART

HYDERABAD, INDIA JUNE 1994
SO I GUESS IT BECOMES A QUESTION OF "WHAT IS" AND "WHAT ISN'T" - AND I DARE NOT BE SO SARCASTIC IN FRONT OF YG ...
ANAND: DO YOU LOVE ME? MUST THERE BE WORDS TO COME BETWEEN US?
THE END (FOR NOW AT LEAST)

A young Indian-American man living in NYC agrees to an arranged marriage with an Indian woman he's never met. As the wedding date nears, he flirts with several other women—including his therapist, neighbor, and colleague—while dreaming of a life of freedom and free will.

www.ingramcontent.com/pod-product-compliance
Lightning Source LLC
La Vergne TN
LVHW050549160826
845677LV00011B/2249

* 9 7 9 8 2 2 7 2 0 8 8 2 8 *